CHI- … AND PEY-PEY

SCHOOL DAY DRAMA

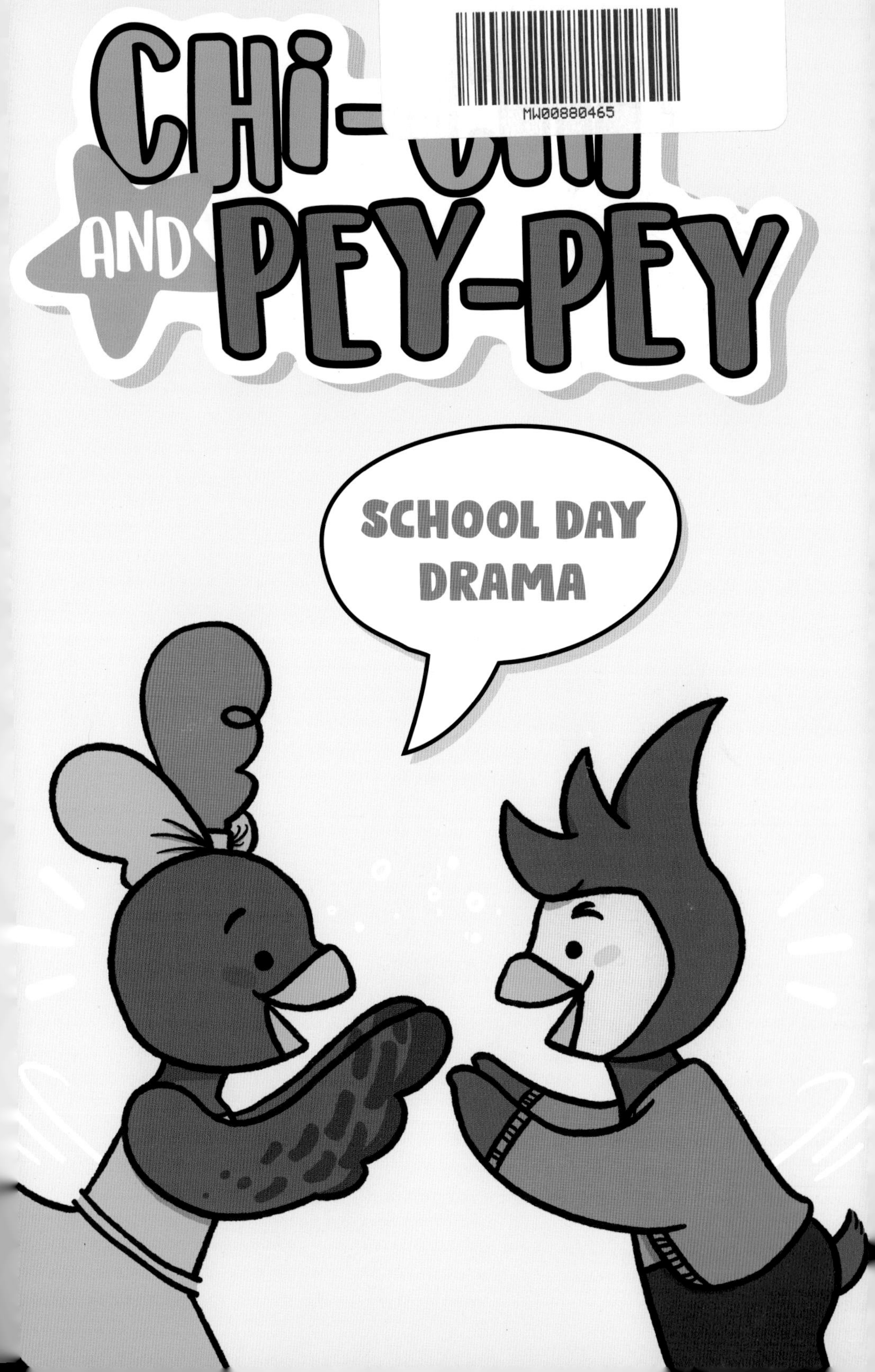

For Serafina, who never wanted to be a chicken —J. F.

To my friends —S. P.

SIMON SPOTLIGHT
An imprint of Simon & Schuster Children's Publishing Division
1230 Avenue of the Americas, New York, New York 10020
This Simon Spotlight edition June 2023
Text copyright © 2023 by Jennifer Fosberry
Illustrations copyright © 2023 by Shiho Pate
All rights reserved, including the right of reproduction in whole or in part in
any form. SIMON SPOTLIGHT, READY-TO-READ, and colophon are registered
trademarks of Simon & Schuster, Inc. For information about special discounts
for bulk purchases, please contact Simon & Schuster Special Sales at
1-866-506-1949 or business@simonandschuster.com.
Manufactured in China 0223 SCP
10 9 8 7 6 5 4 3 2 1
Cataloging-in-Publication Data for this title is available from the Library of
Congress.
ISBN 978-1-6659-3189-2 (hc)
ISBN 978-1-6659-3188-5 (pbk)
ISBN 978-1-6659-3190-8 (ebook)

CHI-CHI AND PEY-PEY

SCHOOL DAY DRAMA

Written by **Jennifer Fosberry**
Illustrated by **Shiho Pate**

Ready-to-Read *GRAPHICS*

Simon Spotlight
New York London Toronto Sydney New Delhi

HOW TO READ THiS BOOK

Chi-Chi and Pey-Pey are here to give you some tips on reading this book.

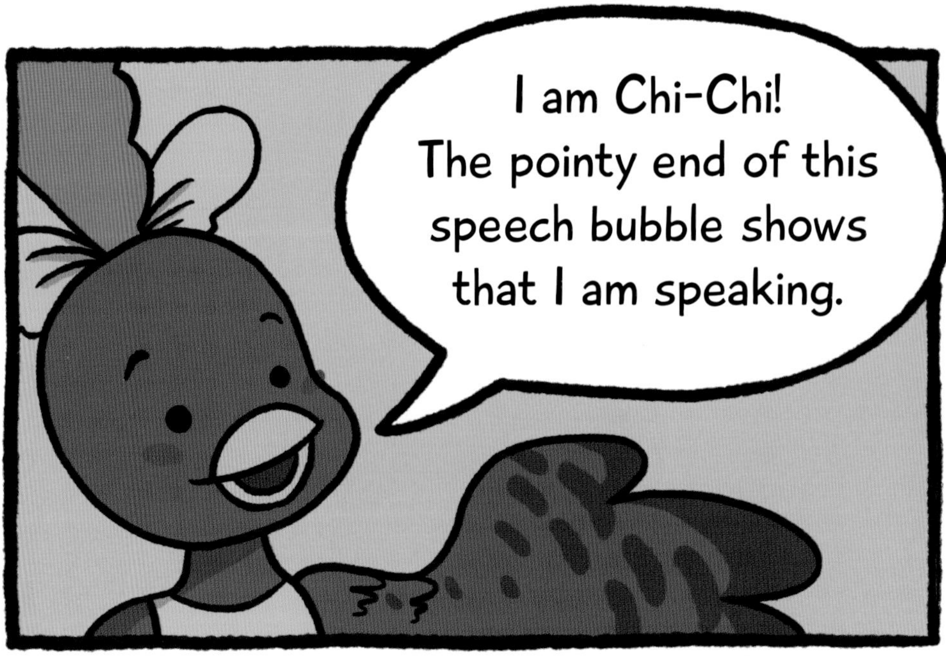
I am Chi-Chi!
The pointy end of this speech bubble shows that I am speaking.

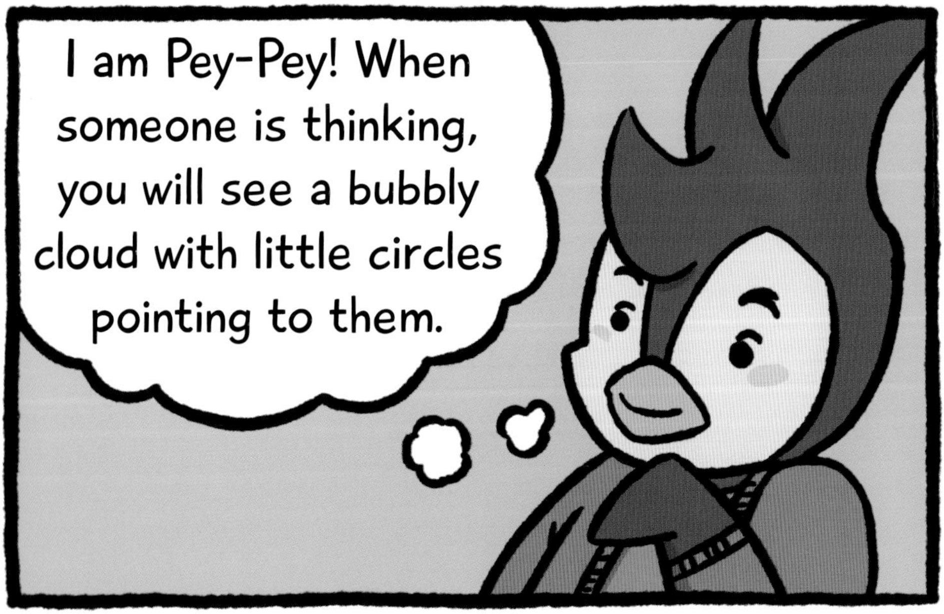
I am Pey-Pey! When someone is thinking, you will see a bubbly cloud with little circles pointing to them.

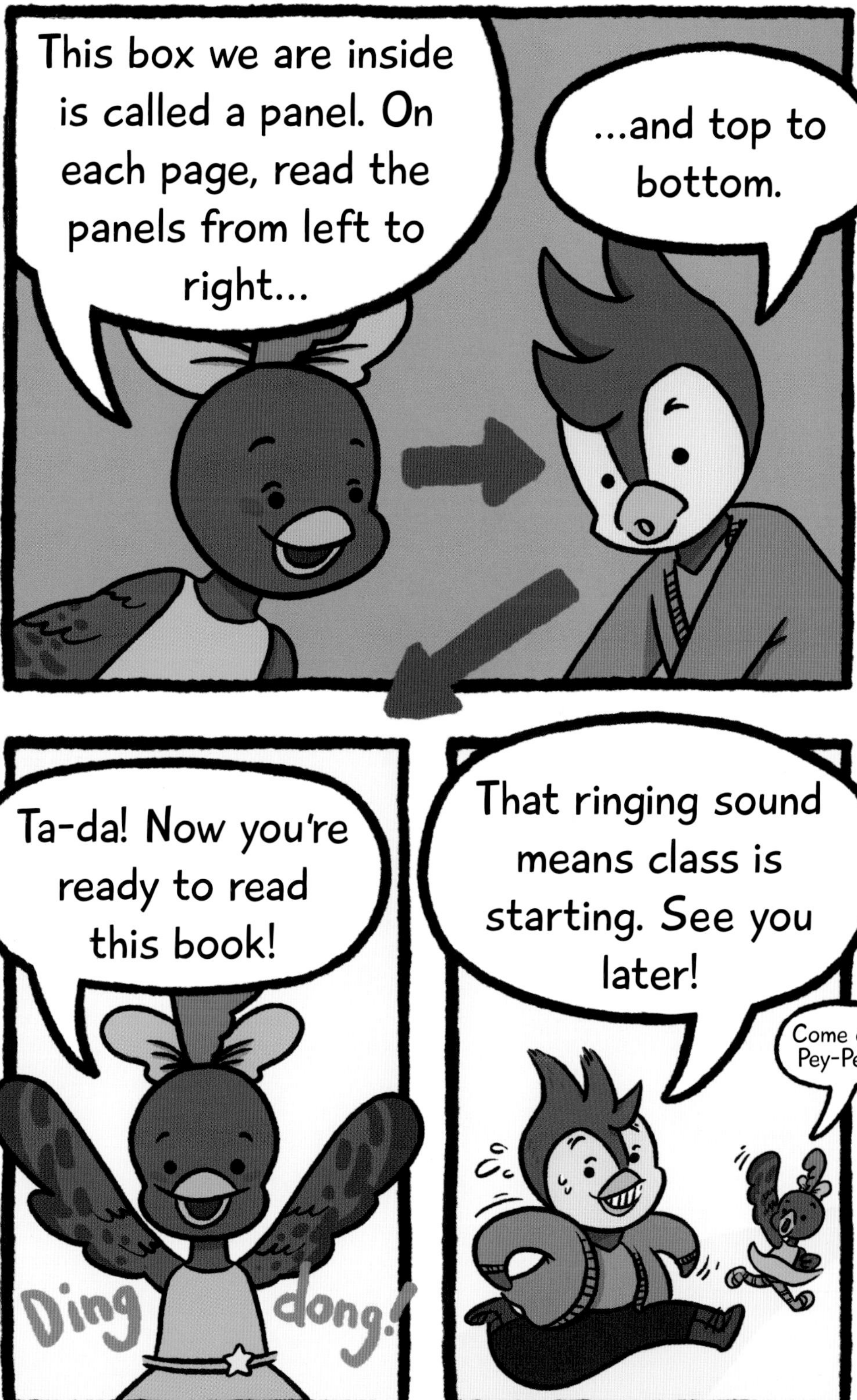
This box we are inside is called a panel. On each page, read the panels from left to right...
...and top to bottom.
Ta-da! Now you're ready to read this book!
Ding dong!
That ringing sound means class is starting. See you later!
Come on, Pey-Pey!

This is Chi-Chi.
Chi-Chi is a chicken.

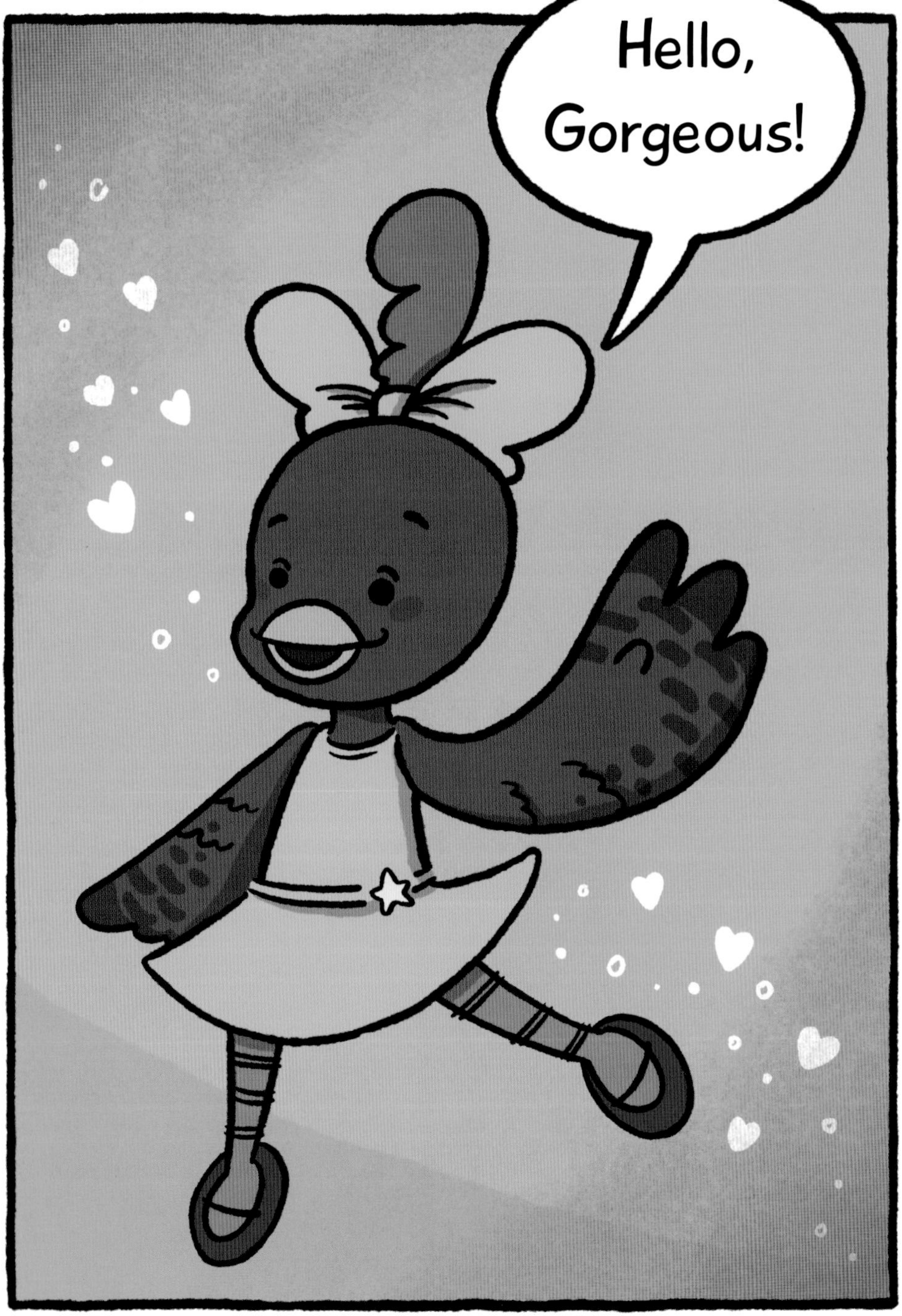
Hello, Gorgeous!

Chi-Chi is the kind of chicken who likes...

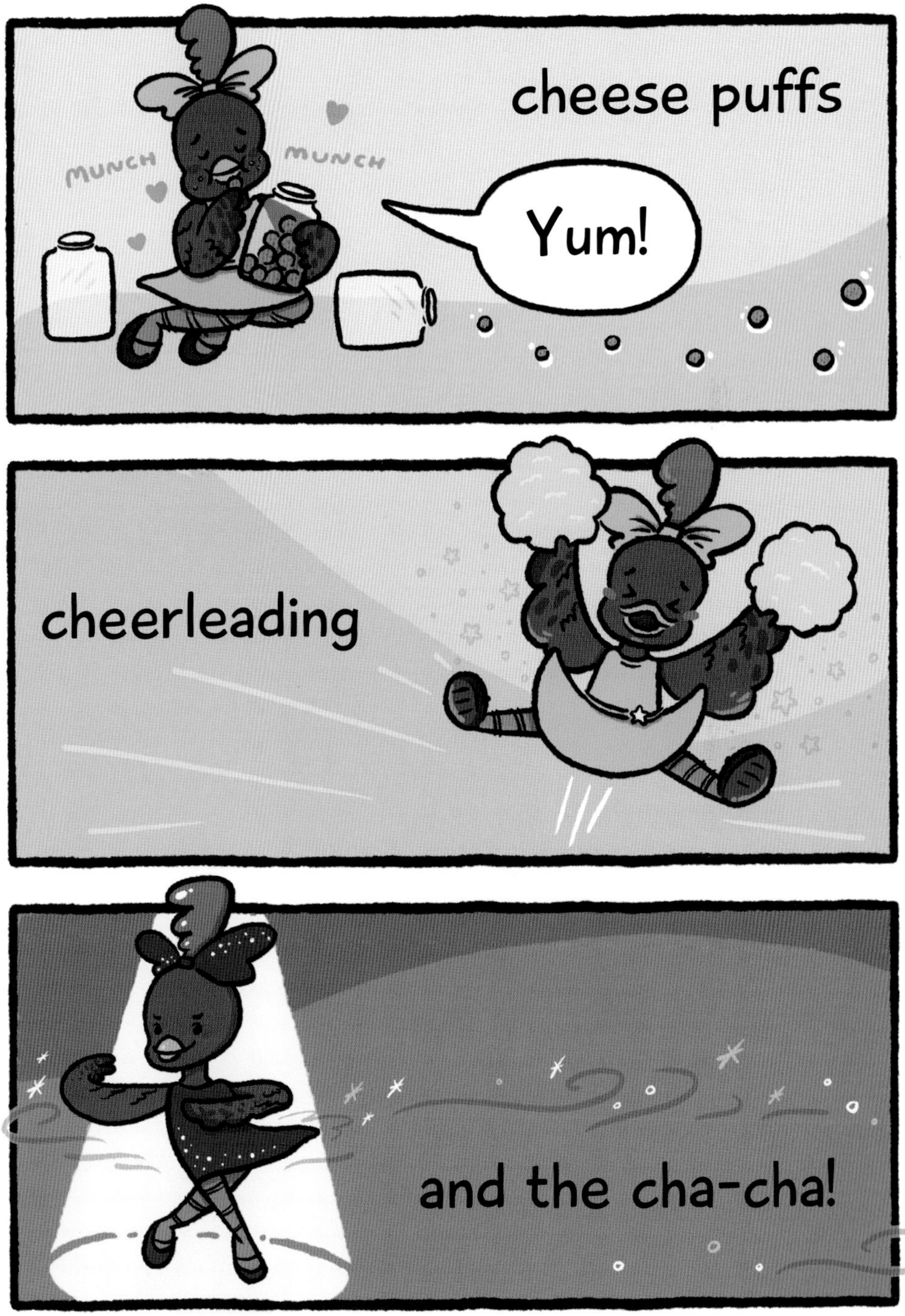
cheese puffs
MUNCH
MUNCH
Yum!
cheerleading
and the cha-cha!

And certainly not the kind of chicken who is worried about the first day of school.

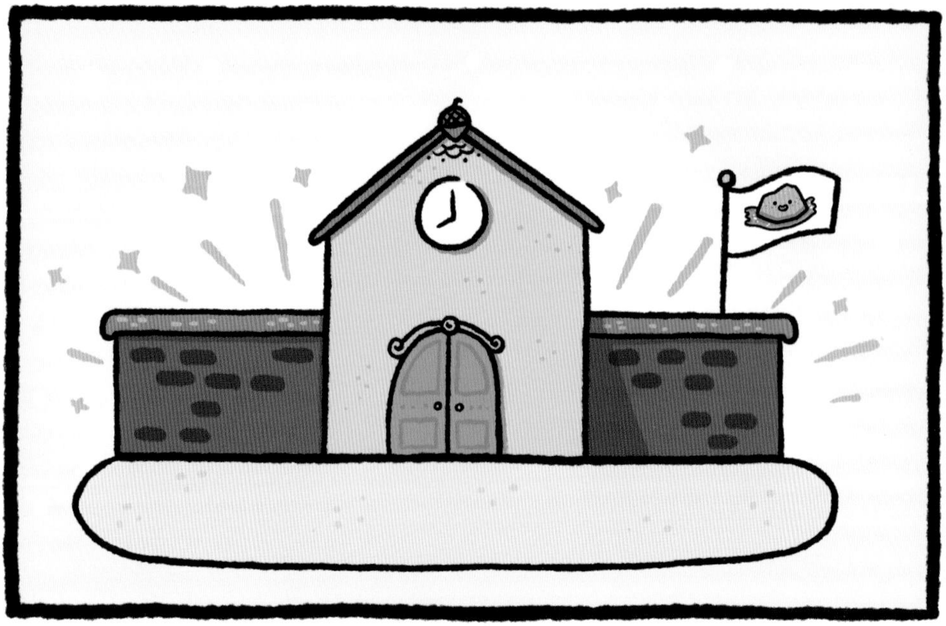

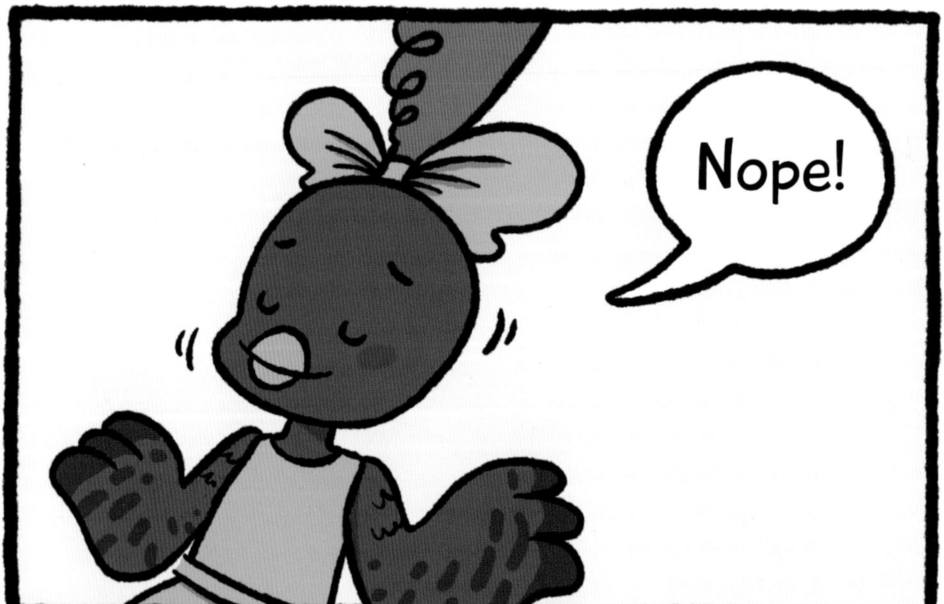
Nope!

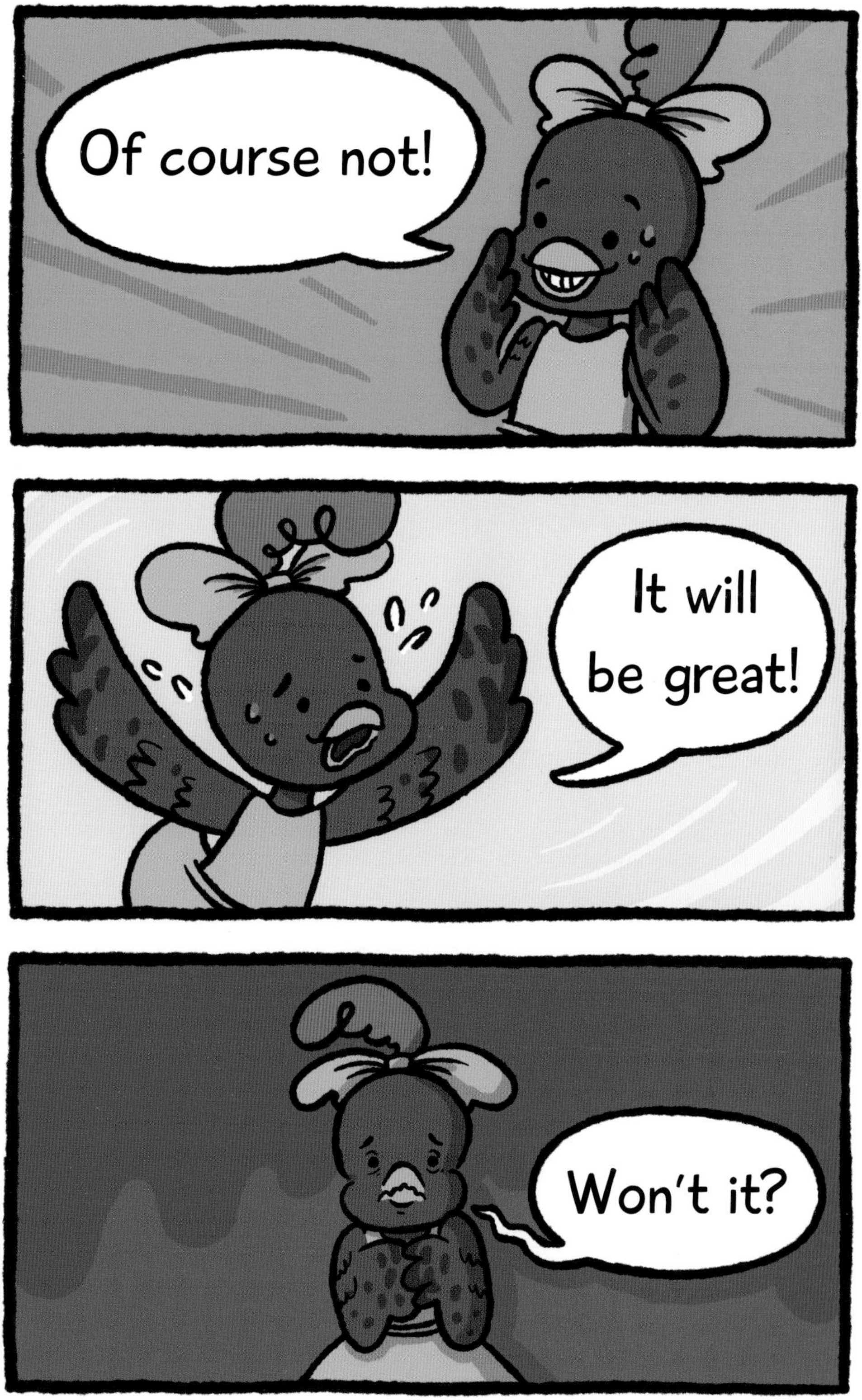
Of course not!
It will be great!
Won't it?

This is Pey-Pey.
Pey-Pey is a penguin.

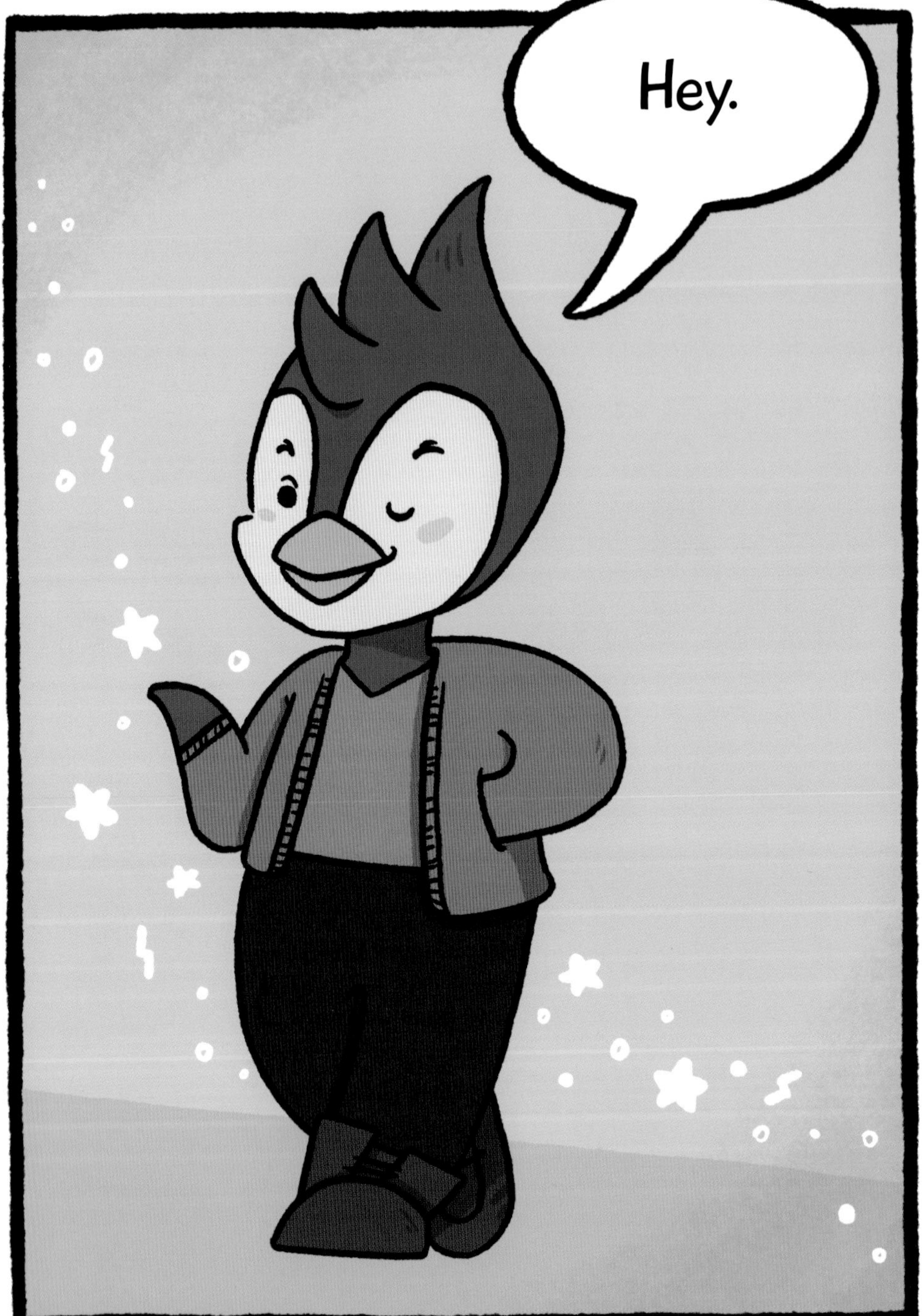
Hey.

Pey-Pey is the kind of penguin who likes...

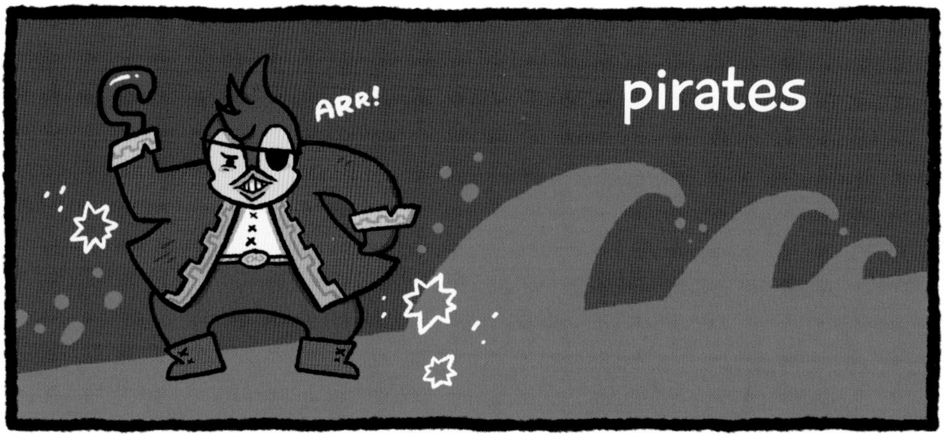
ARR!
pirates

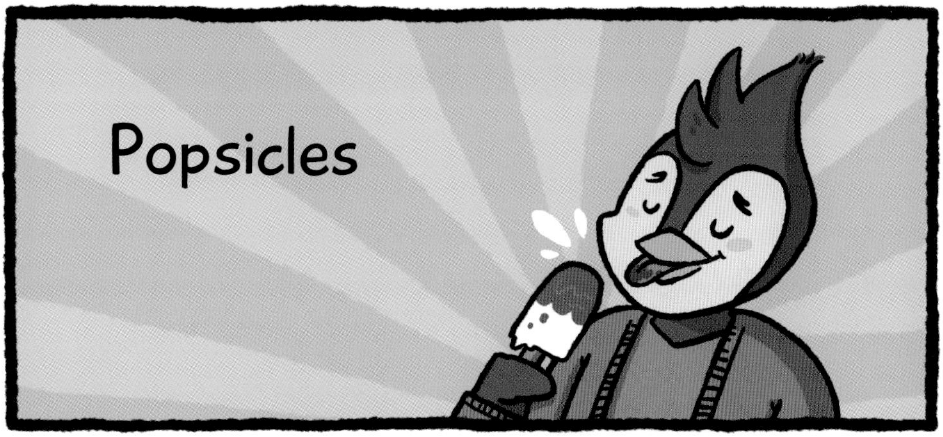
Popsicles

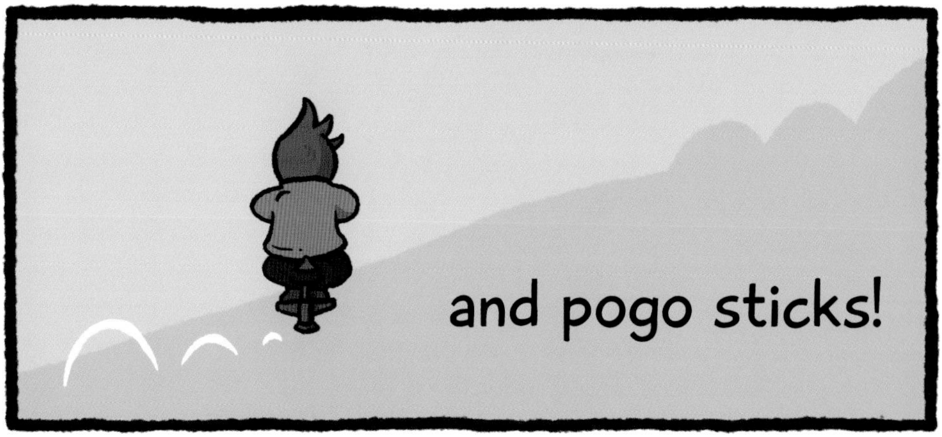
and pogo sticks!

And certainly not the kind of penguin who is nervous about the first day of school.

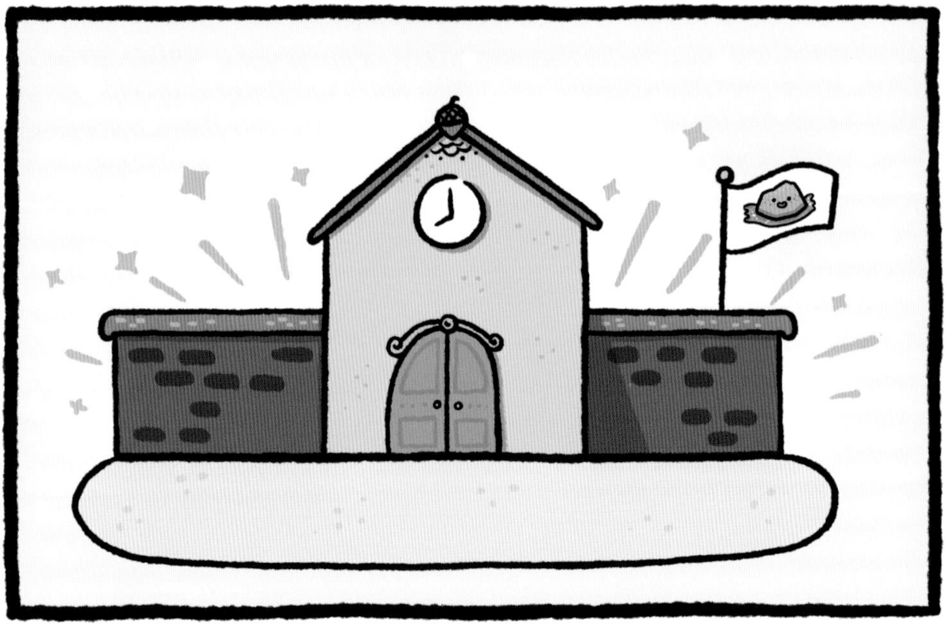

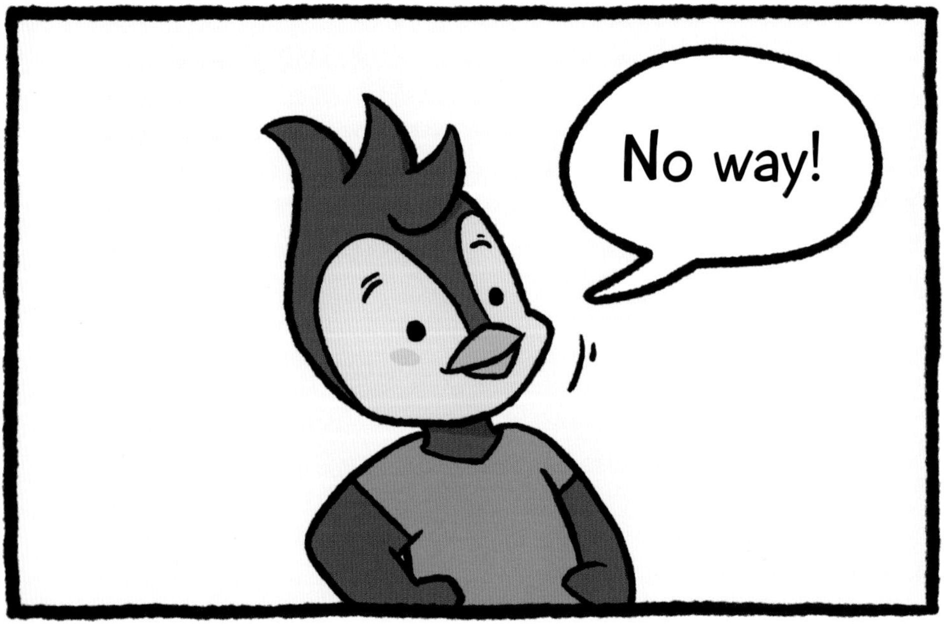
No way!

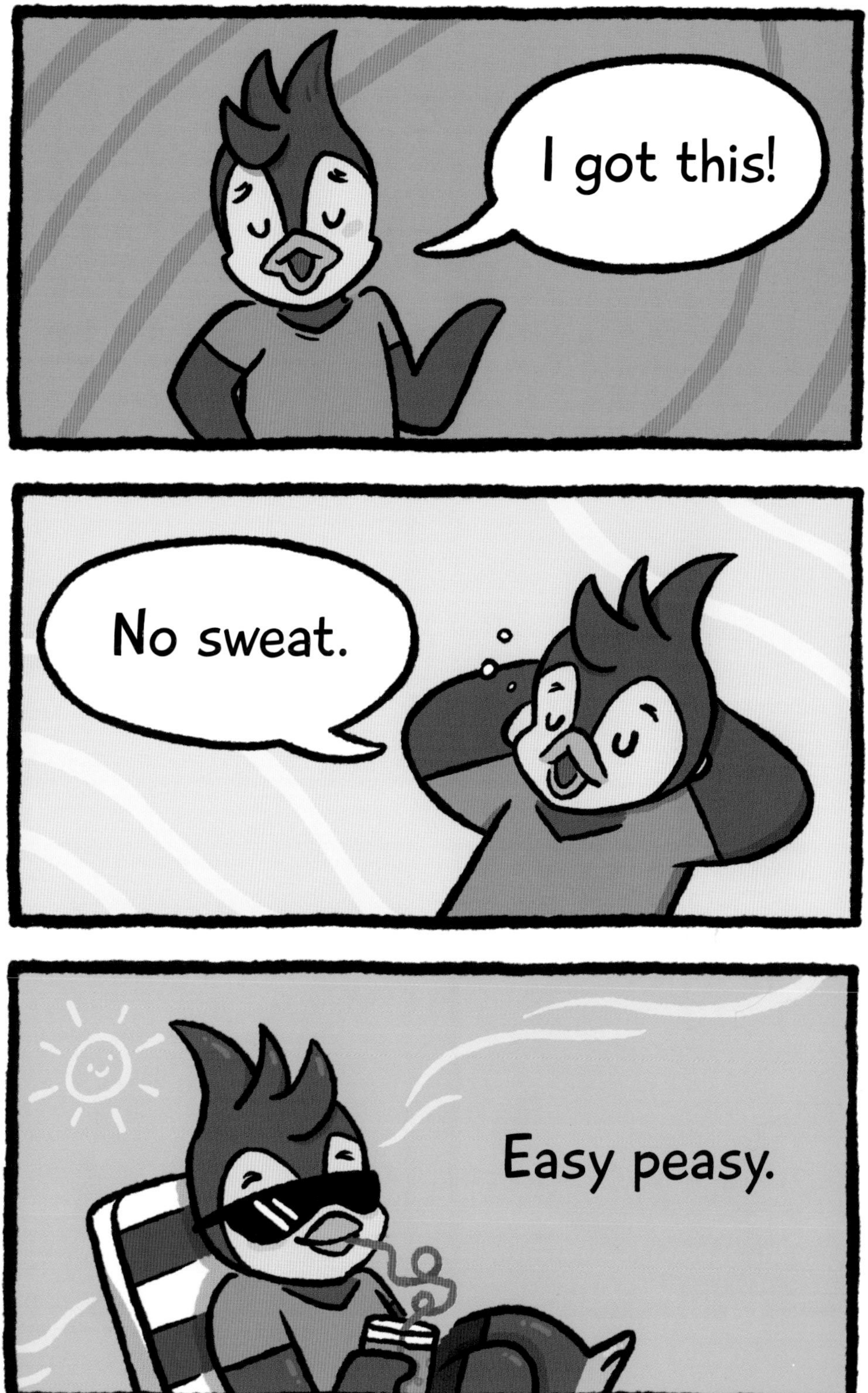
I got this!
No sweat.
Easy peasy.

All summer Chi-Chi prepares for school.

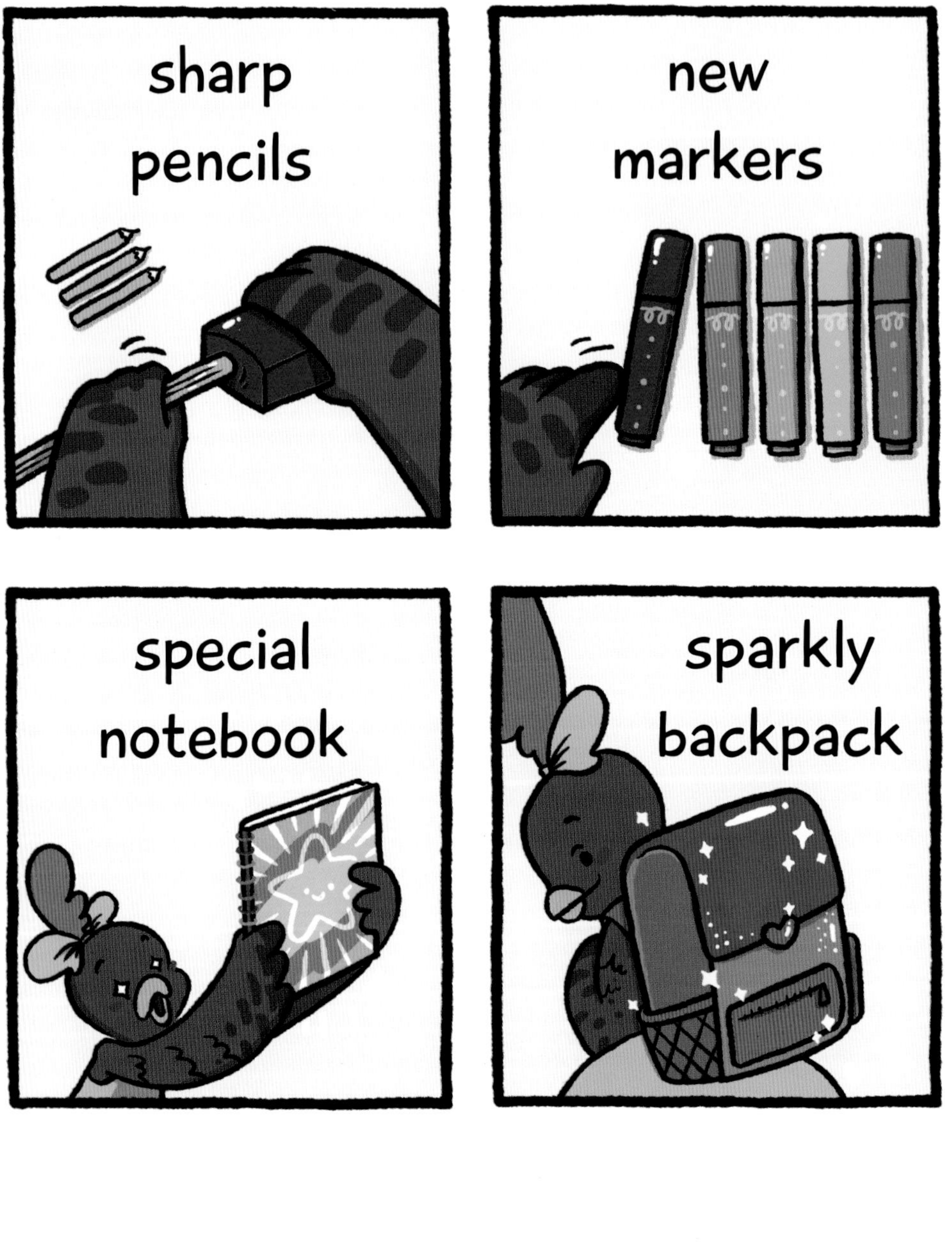
sharp pencils
new markers
special notebook
sparkly backpack

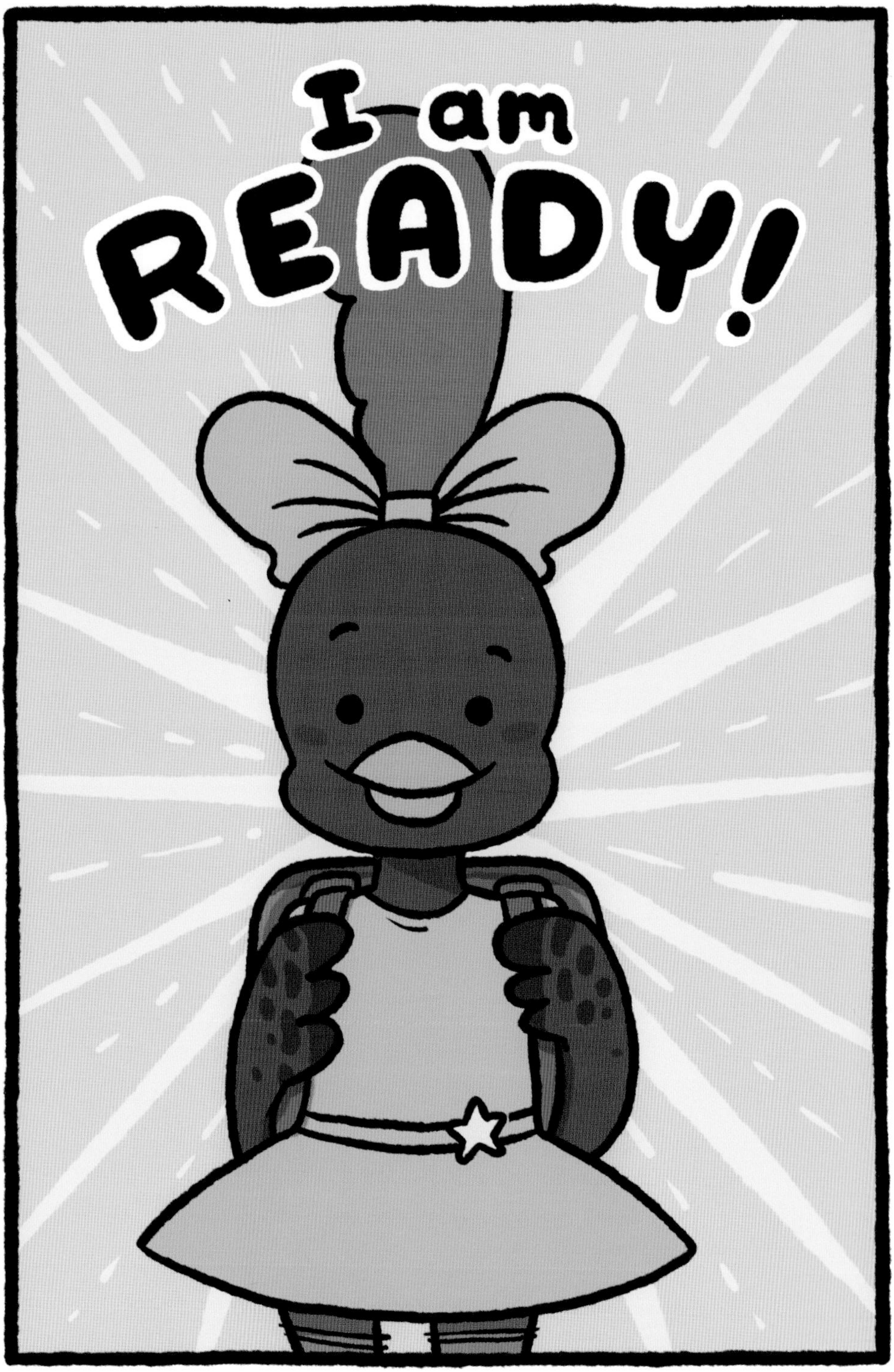
I am READY!

School is still a MONTH away!

All summer Pey-Pey does not prepare for school.

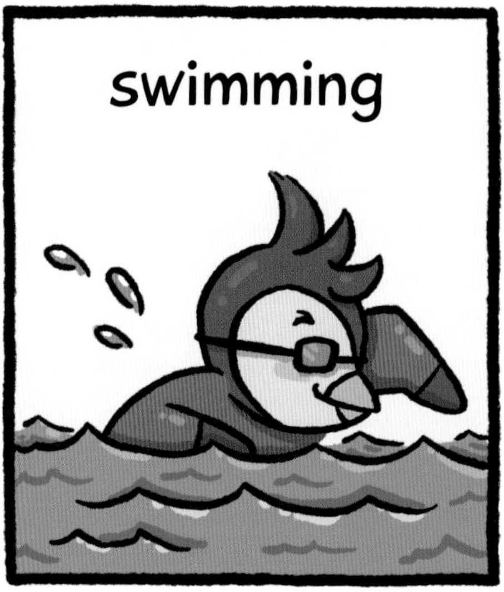
swimming

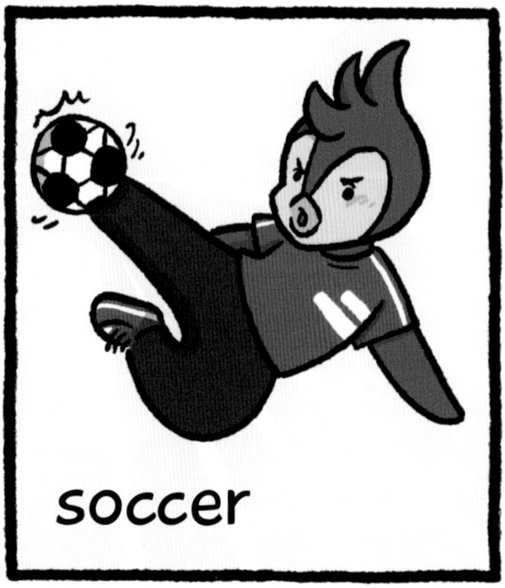
soccer

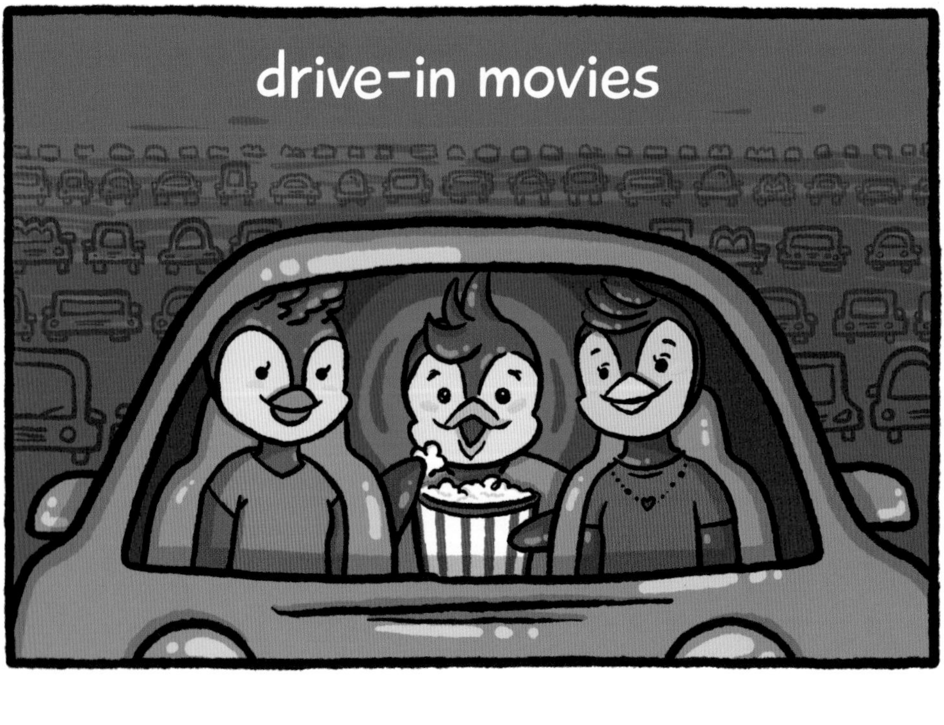
drive-in movies

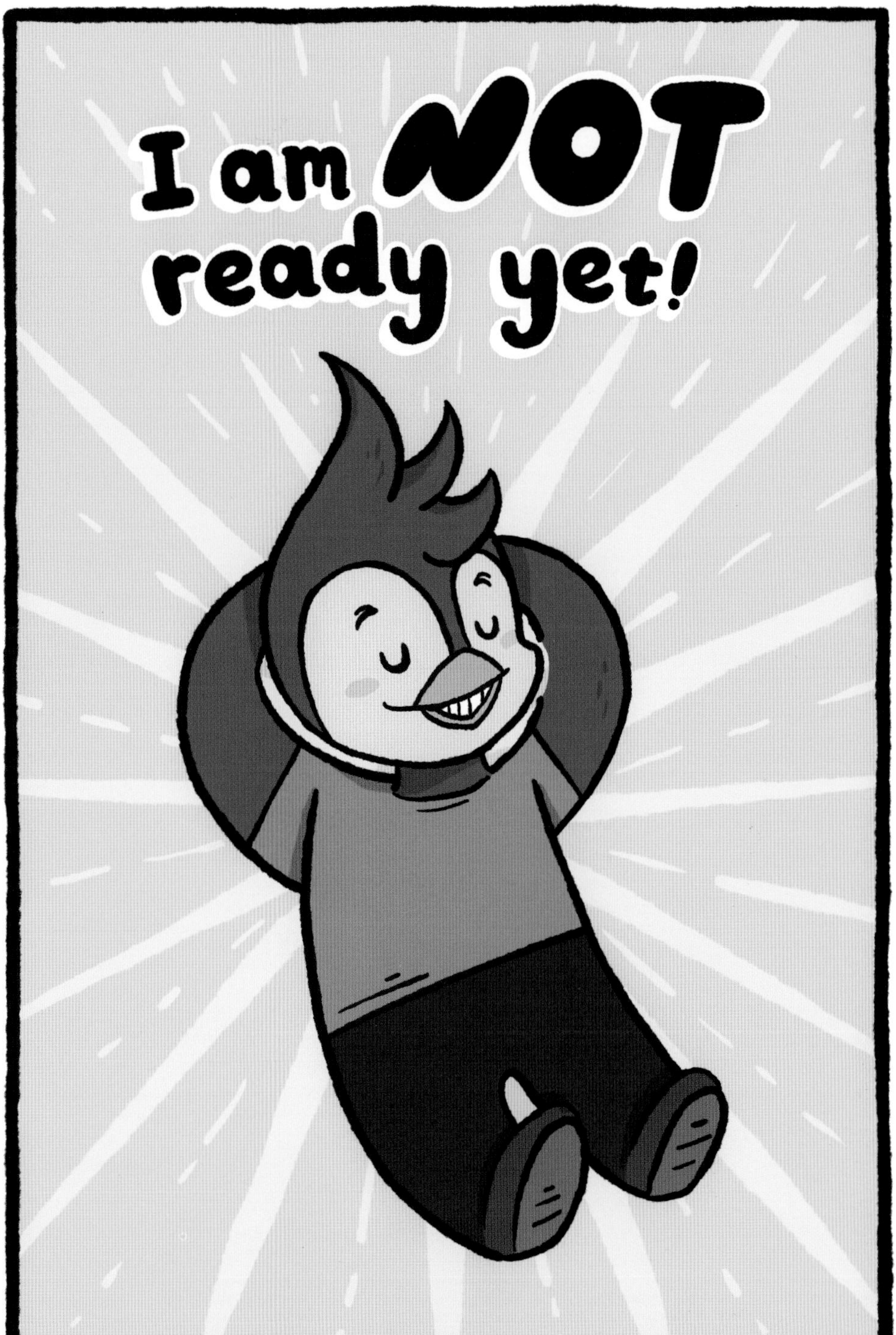
I am NOT ready yet!

School starts TOMORROW!

Chi-Chi has trouble sleeping.

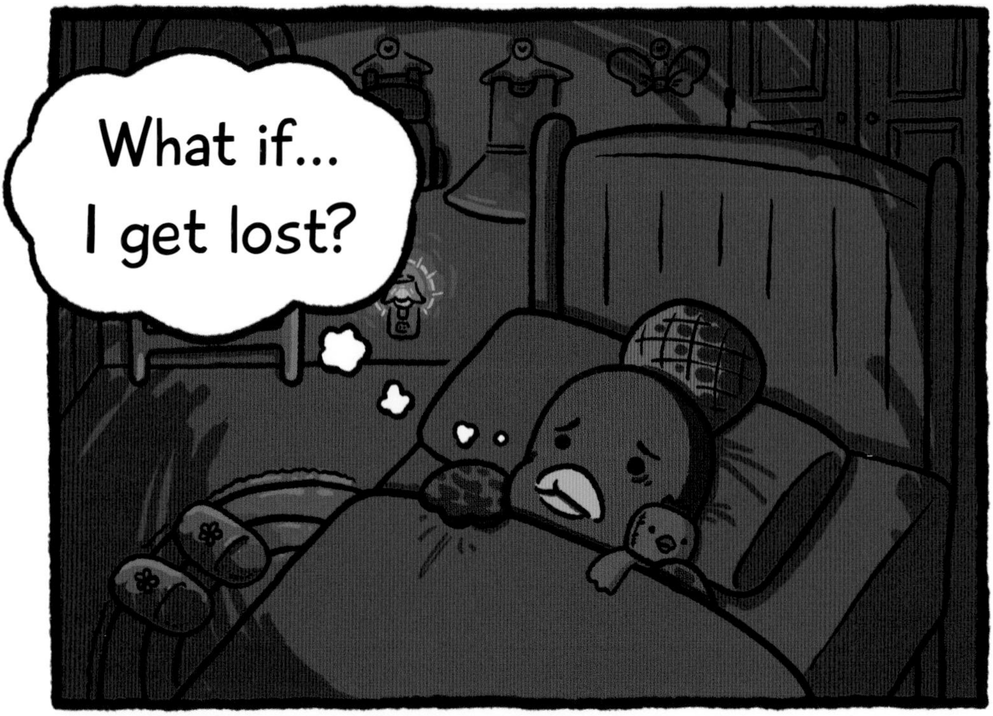
What if... I get lost?

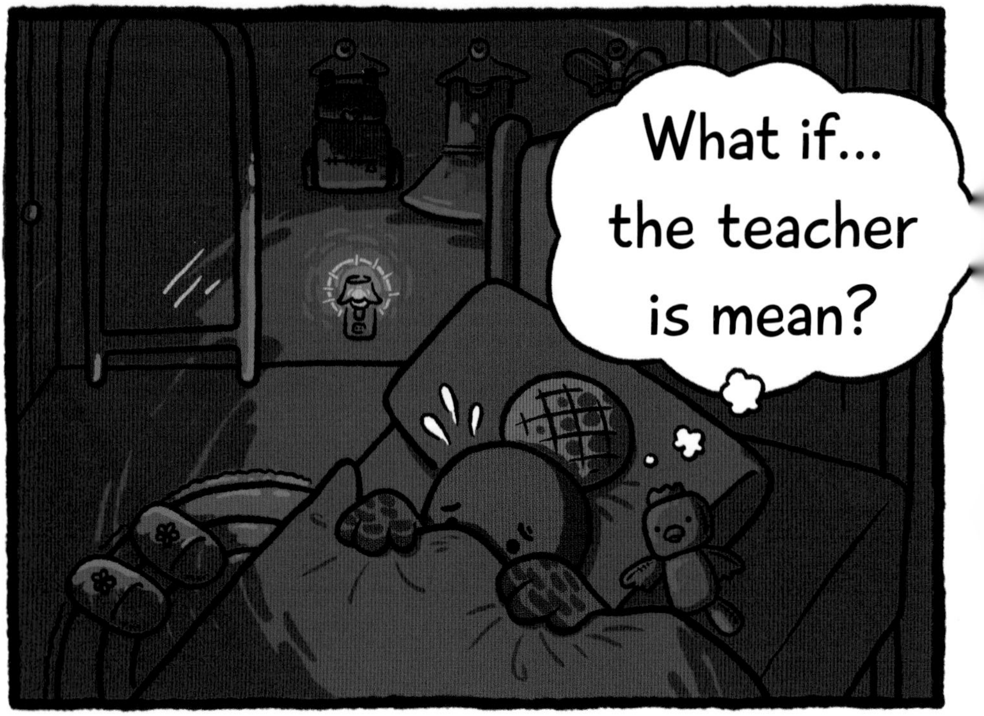
What if... the teacher is mean?

What if...
nobody likes me?

Tell me it will
be OKAY!

Pey-Pey does **NOT** have trouble sleeping.

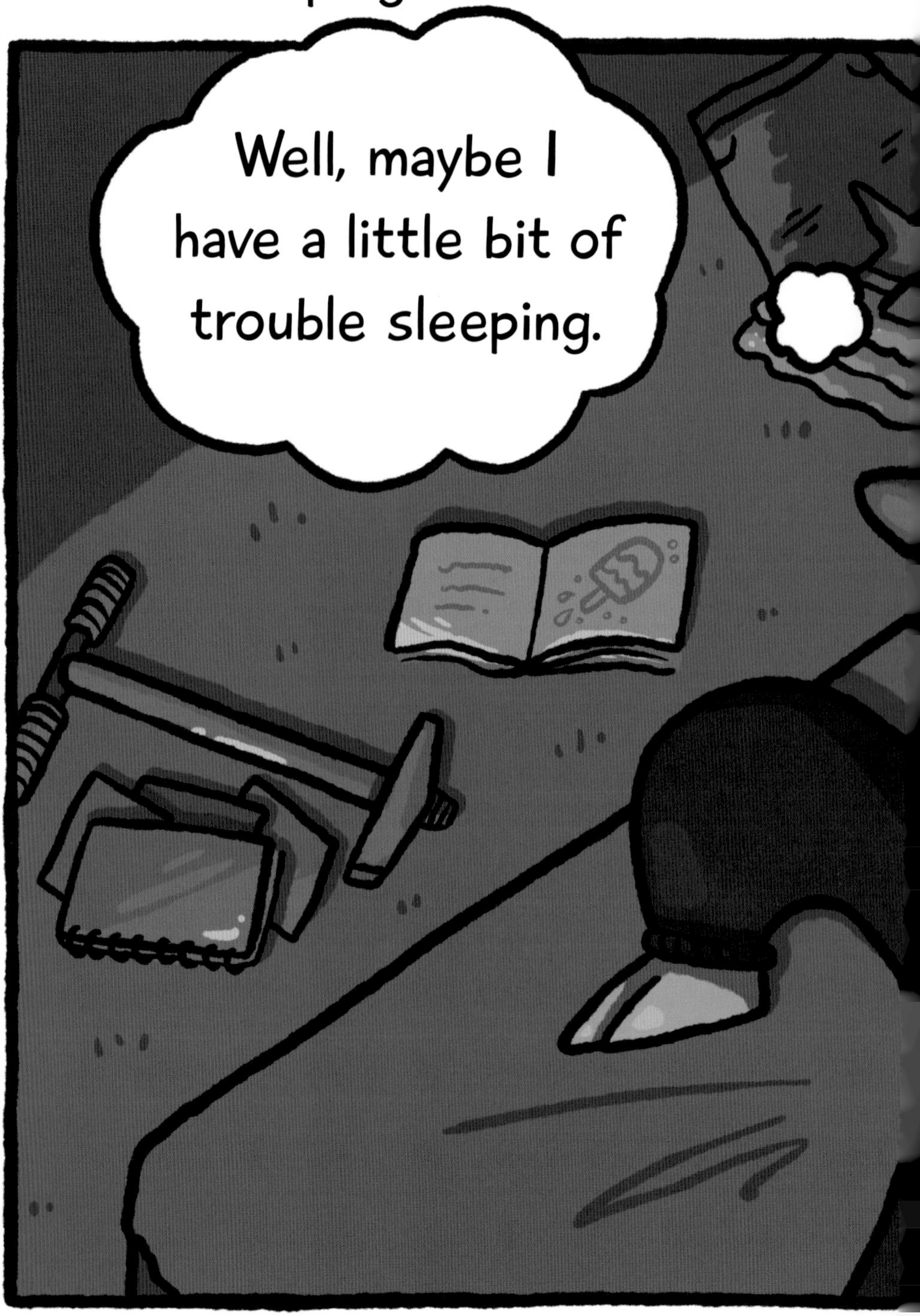
Well, maybe I have a little bit of trouble sleeping.

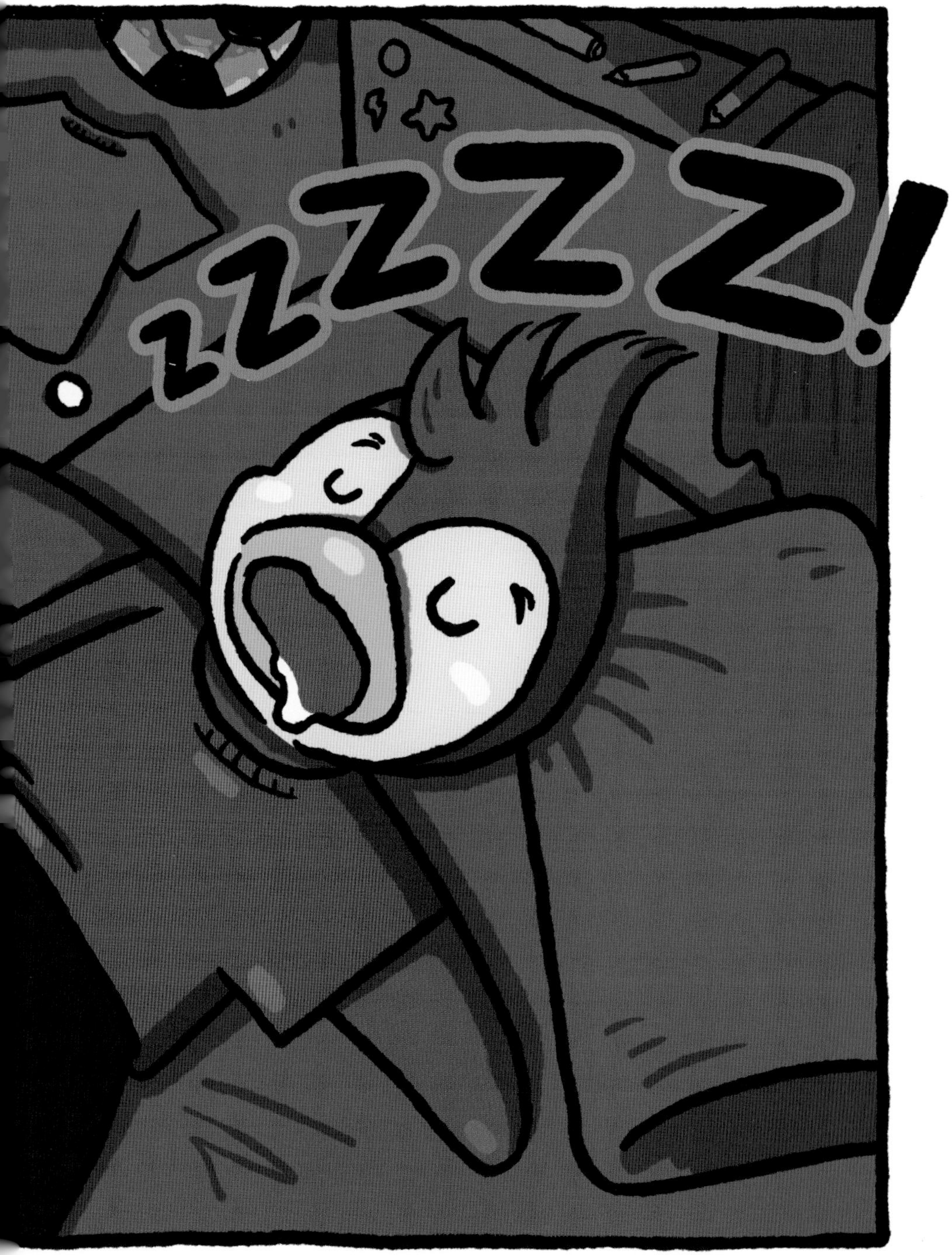

zzzZZZ!

It is the first day of school.

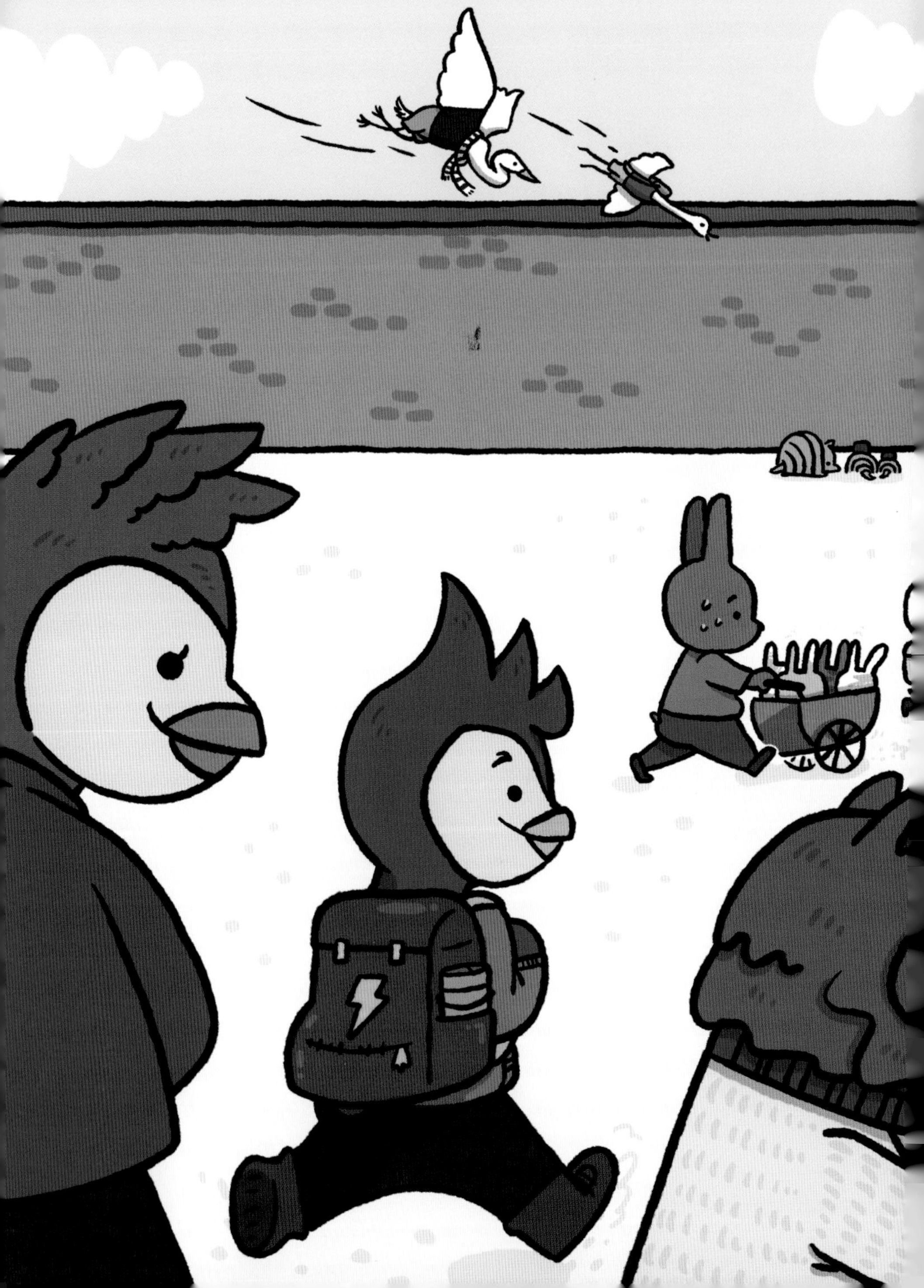

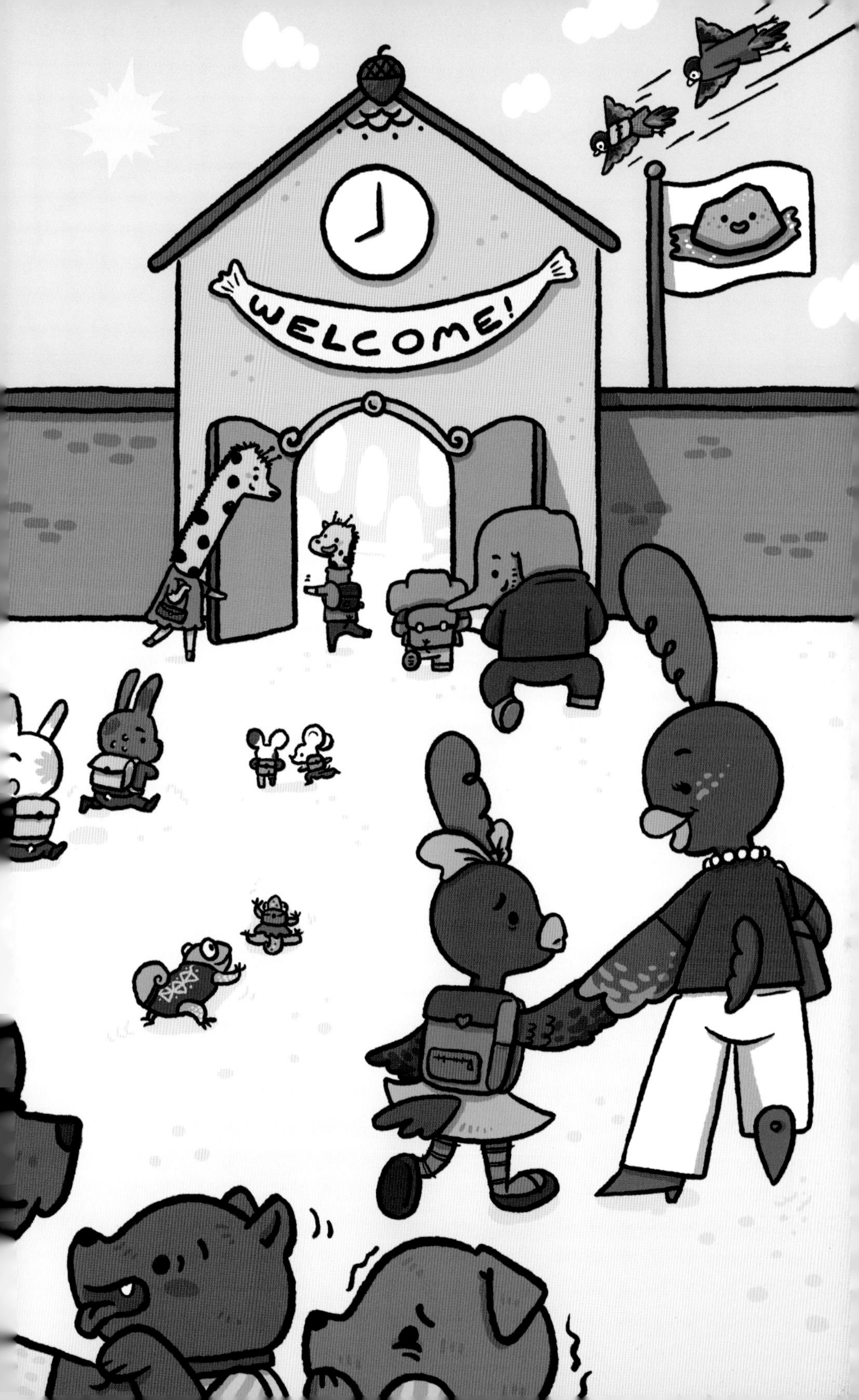
WELCOME!

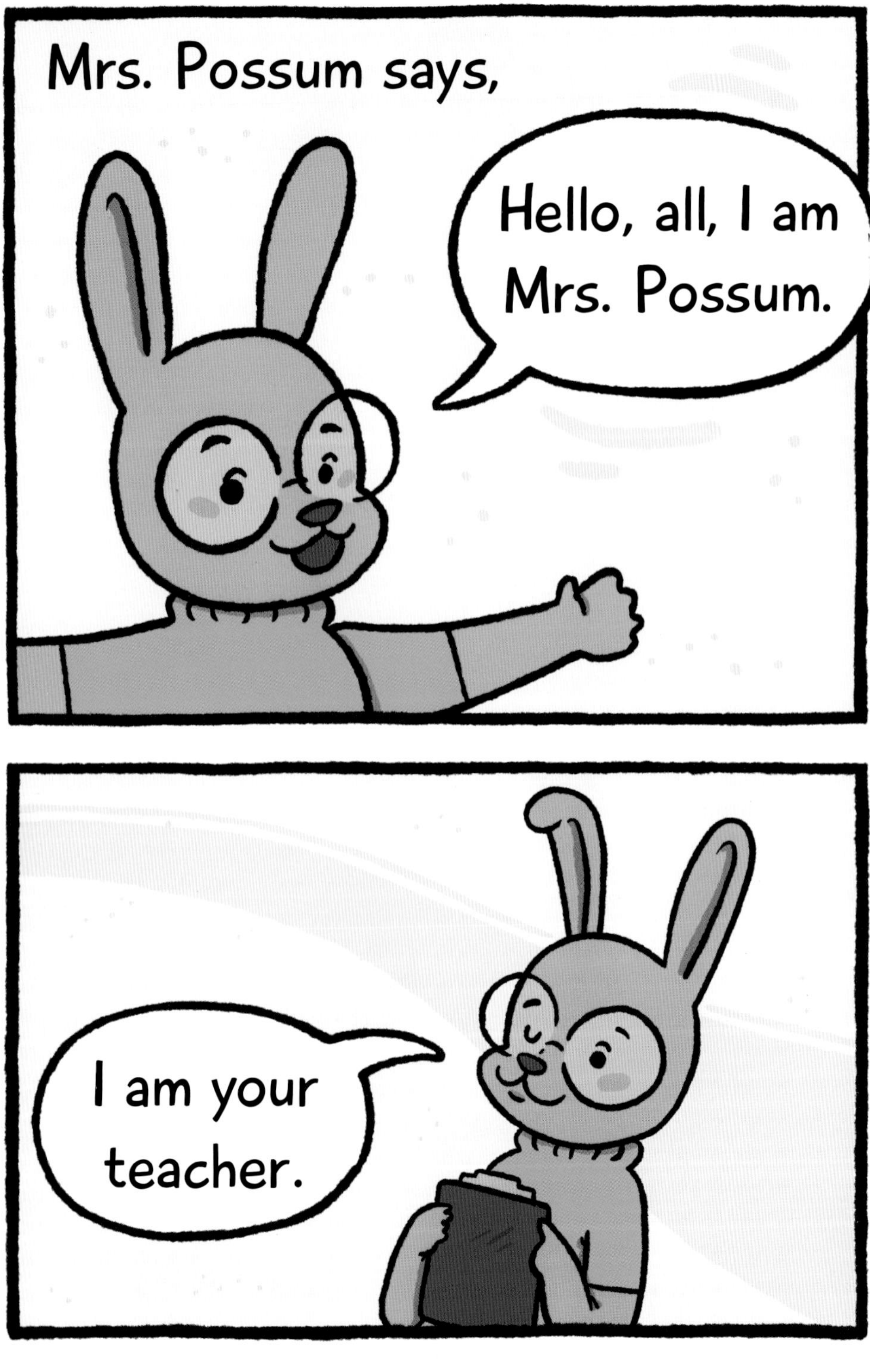
Mrs. Possum says,
Hello, all, I am Mrs. Possum.
I am your teacher.

Mrs. Possum seems nice.

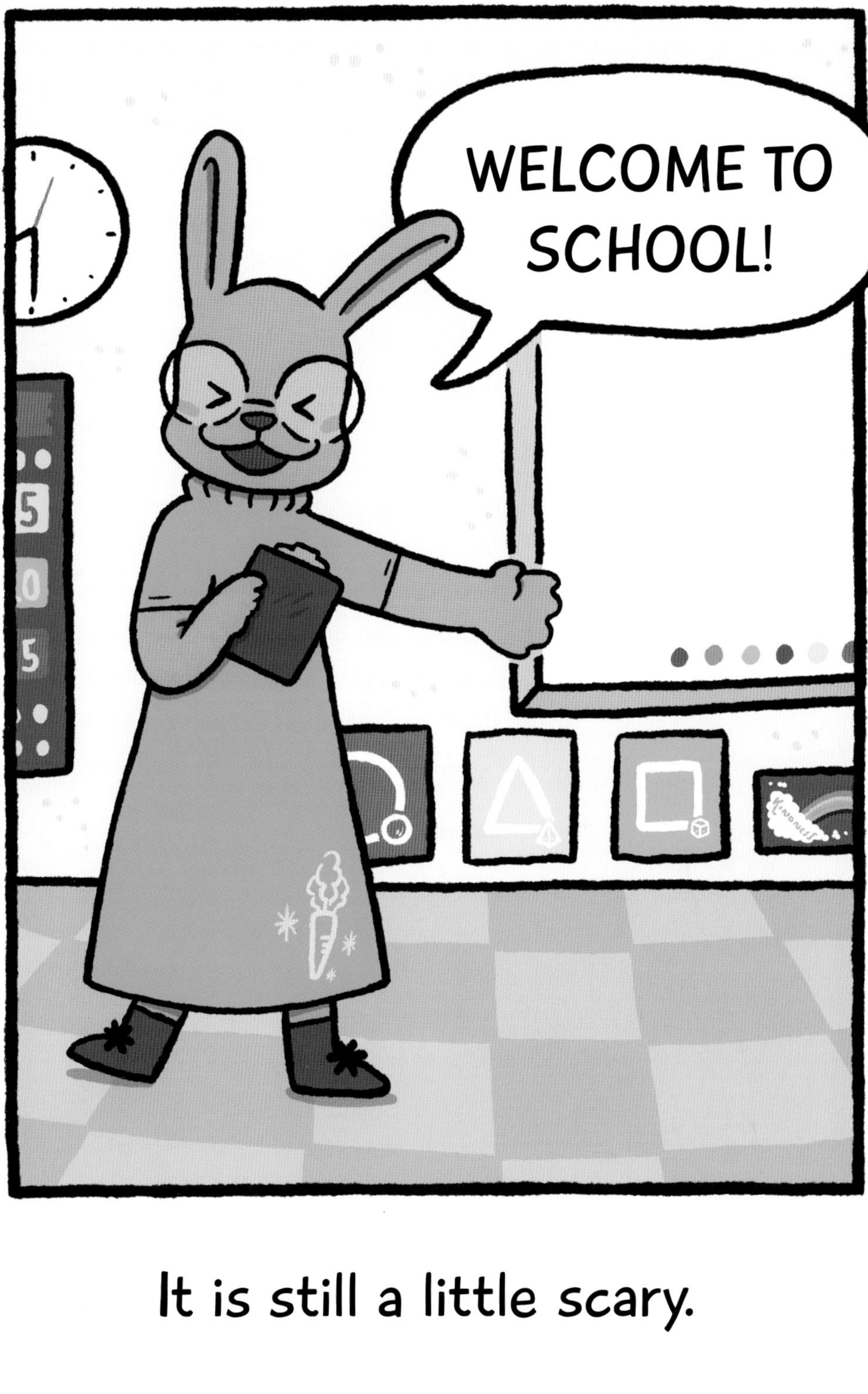
WELCOME TO SCHOOL!

It is still a little scary.

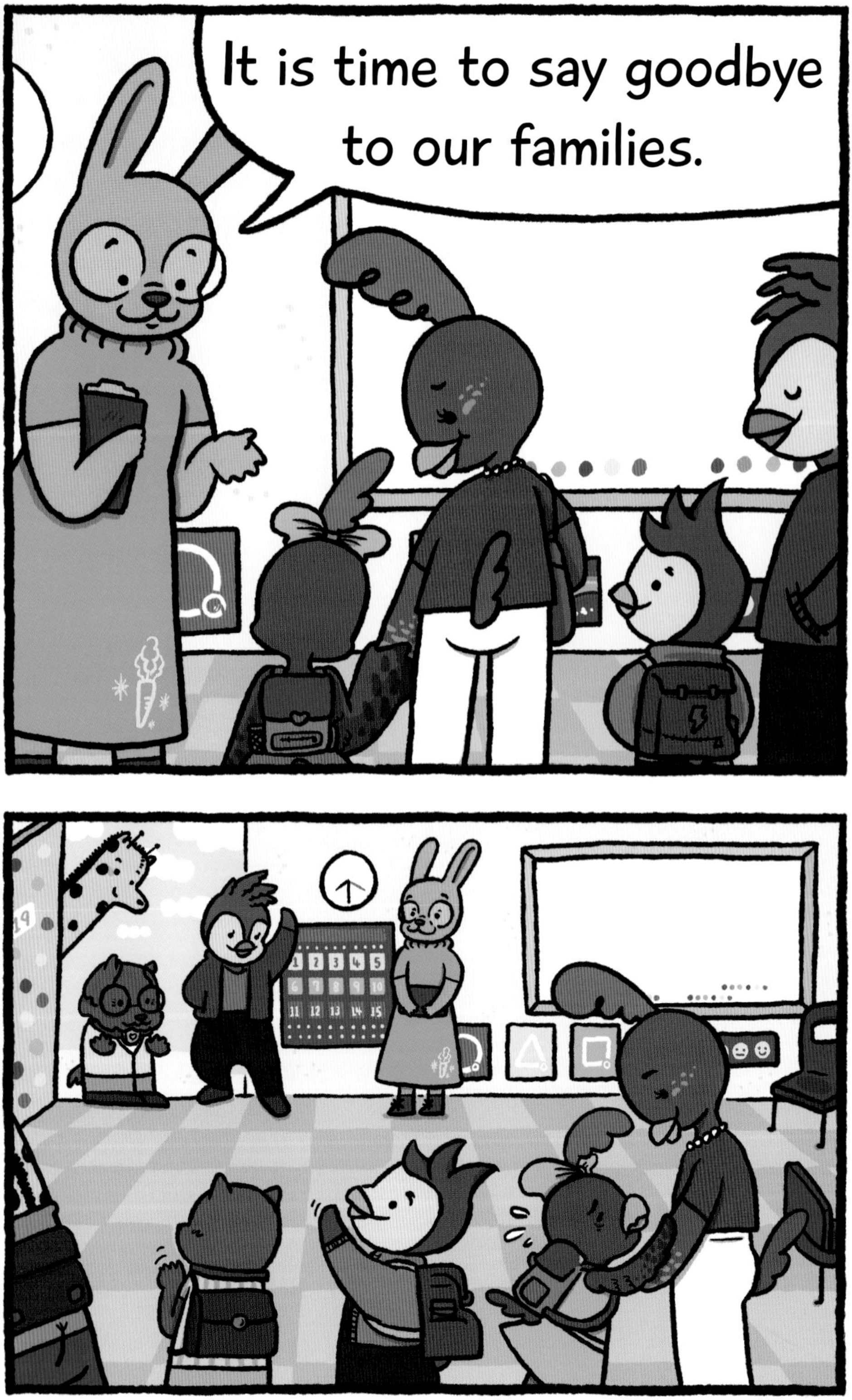
It is time to say goodbye to our families.

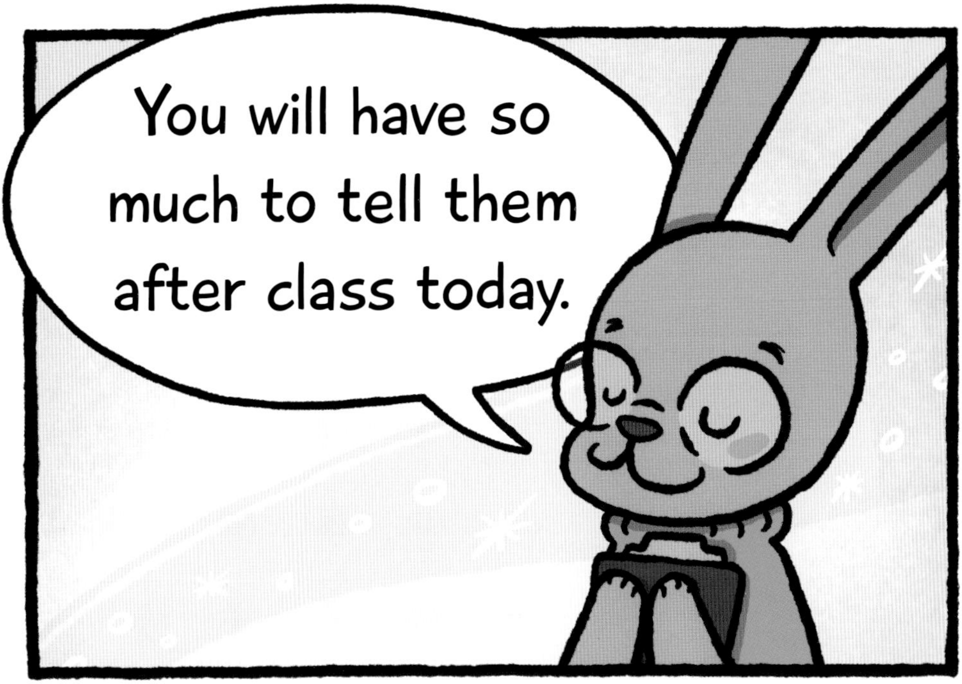
You will have so much to tell them after class today.

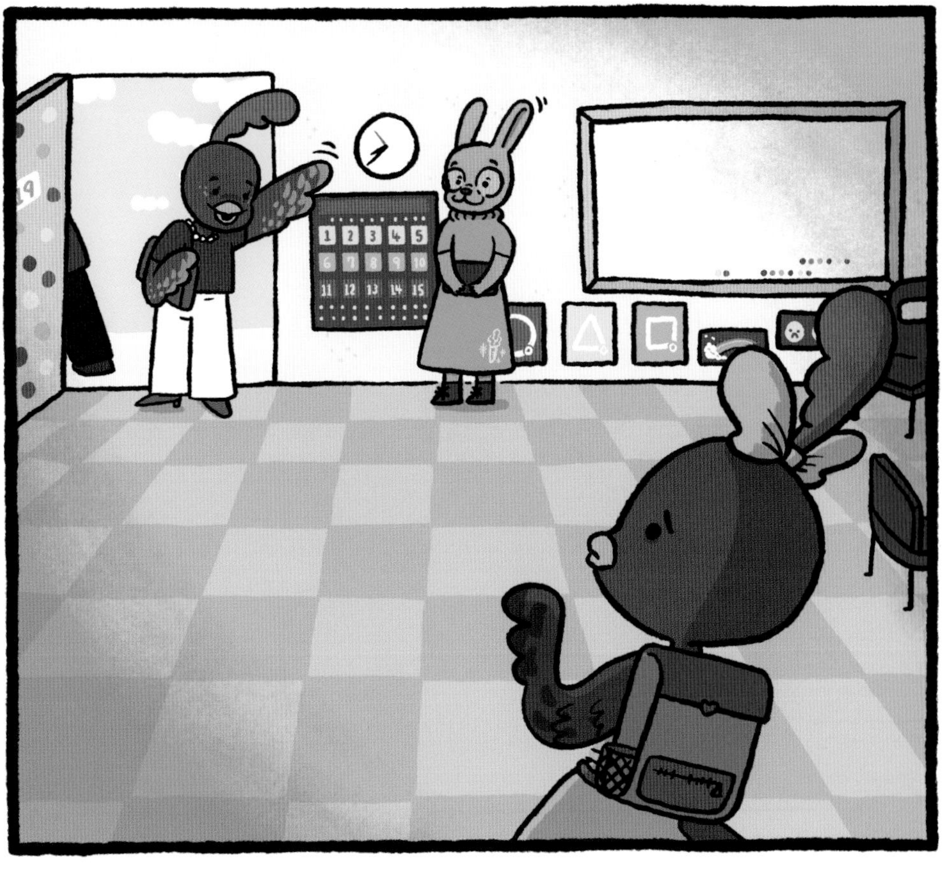

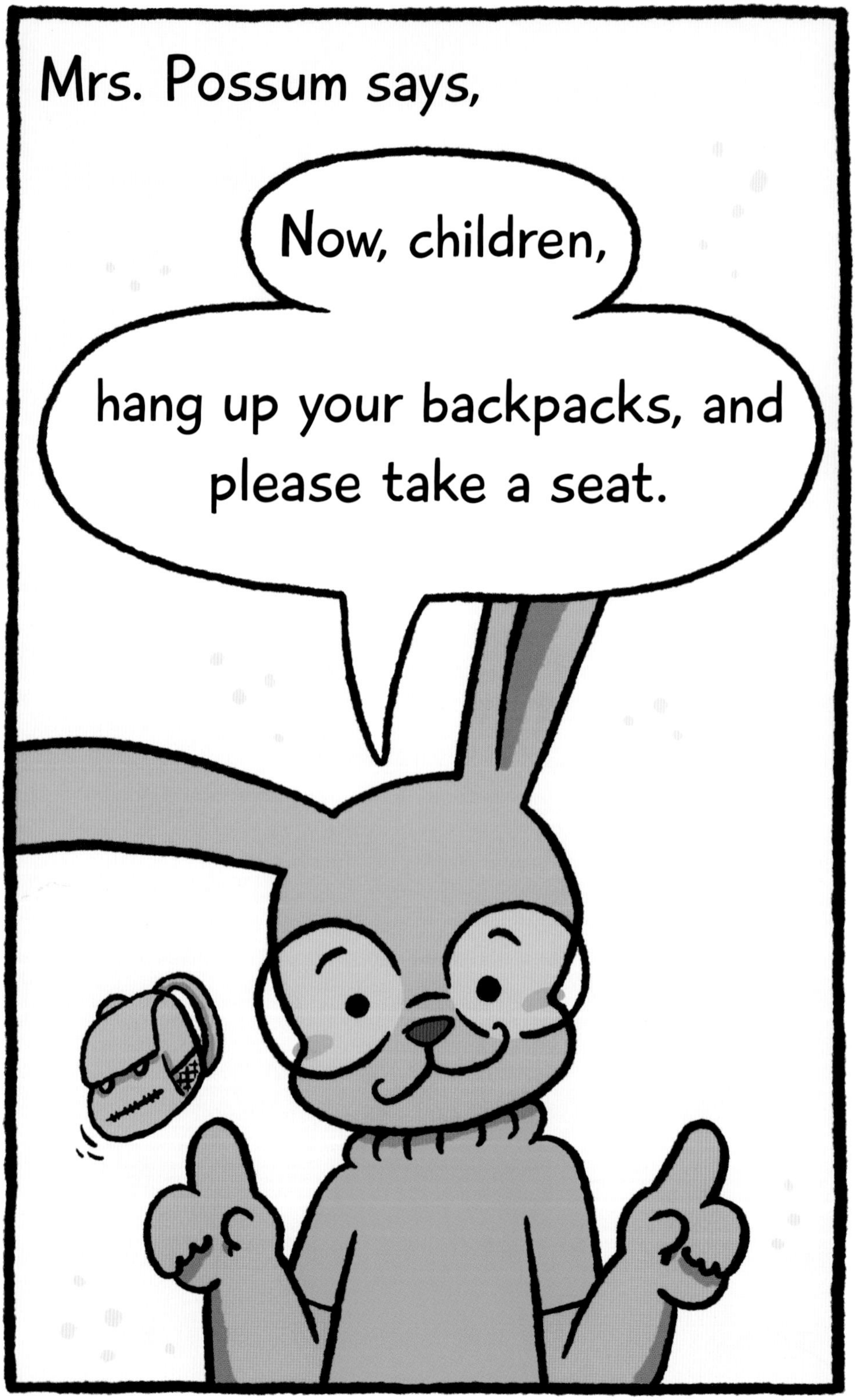
Mrs. Possum says,
Now, children,
hang up your backpacks, and please take a seat.

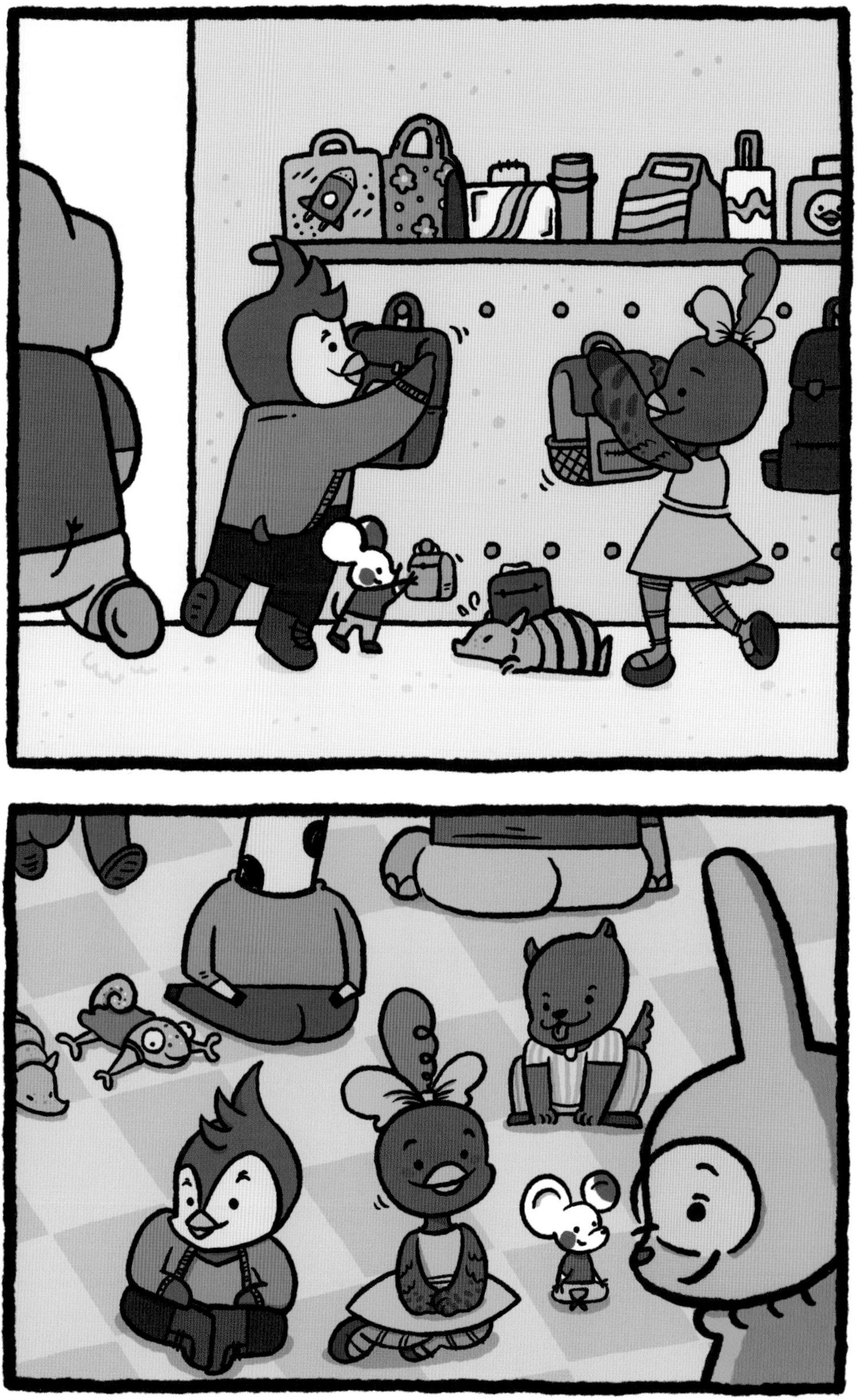

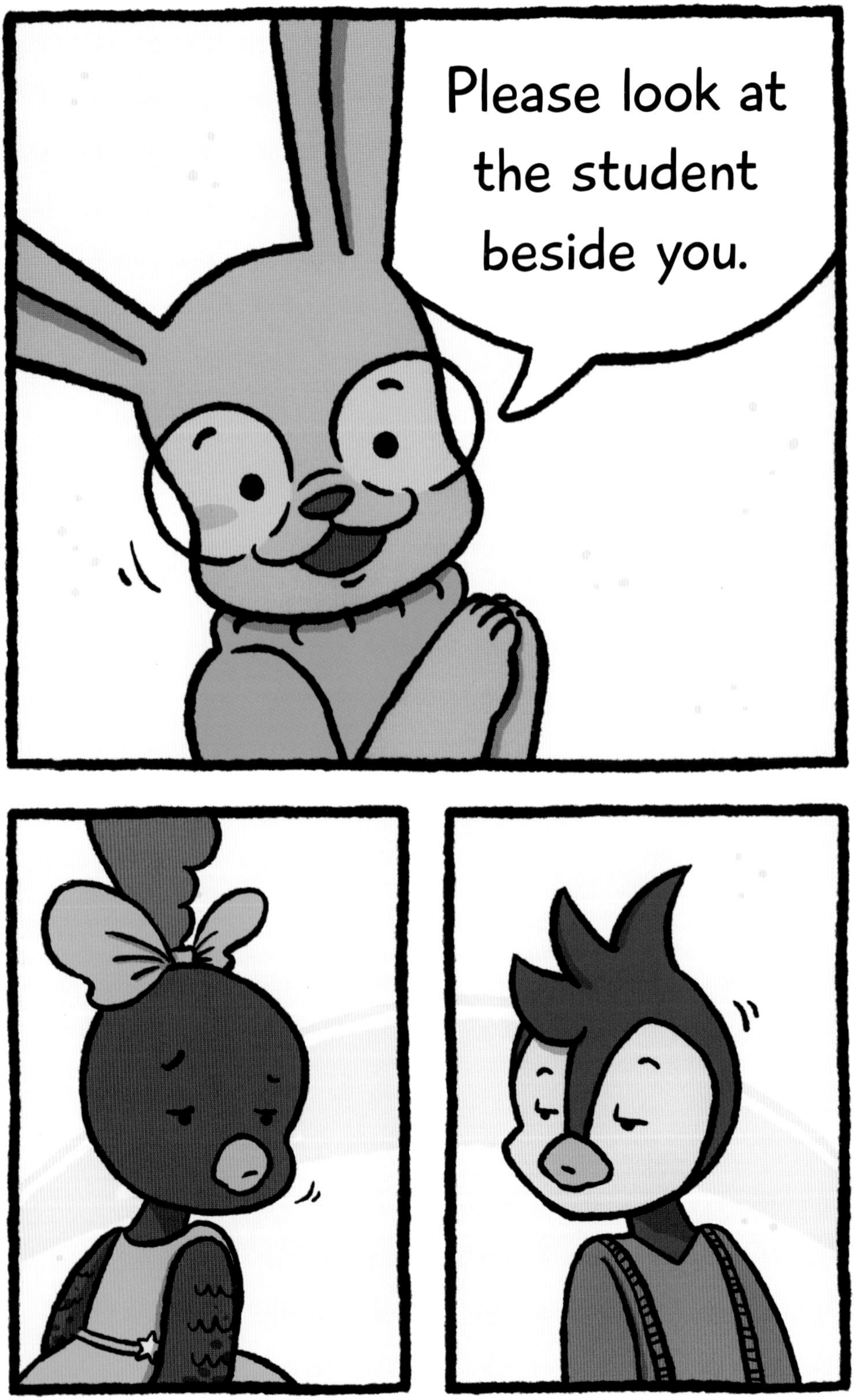
Please look at the student beside you.

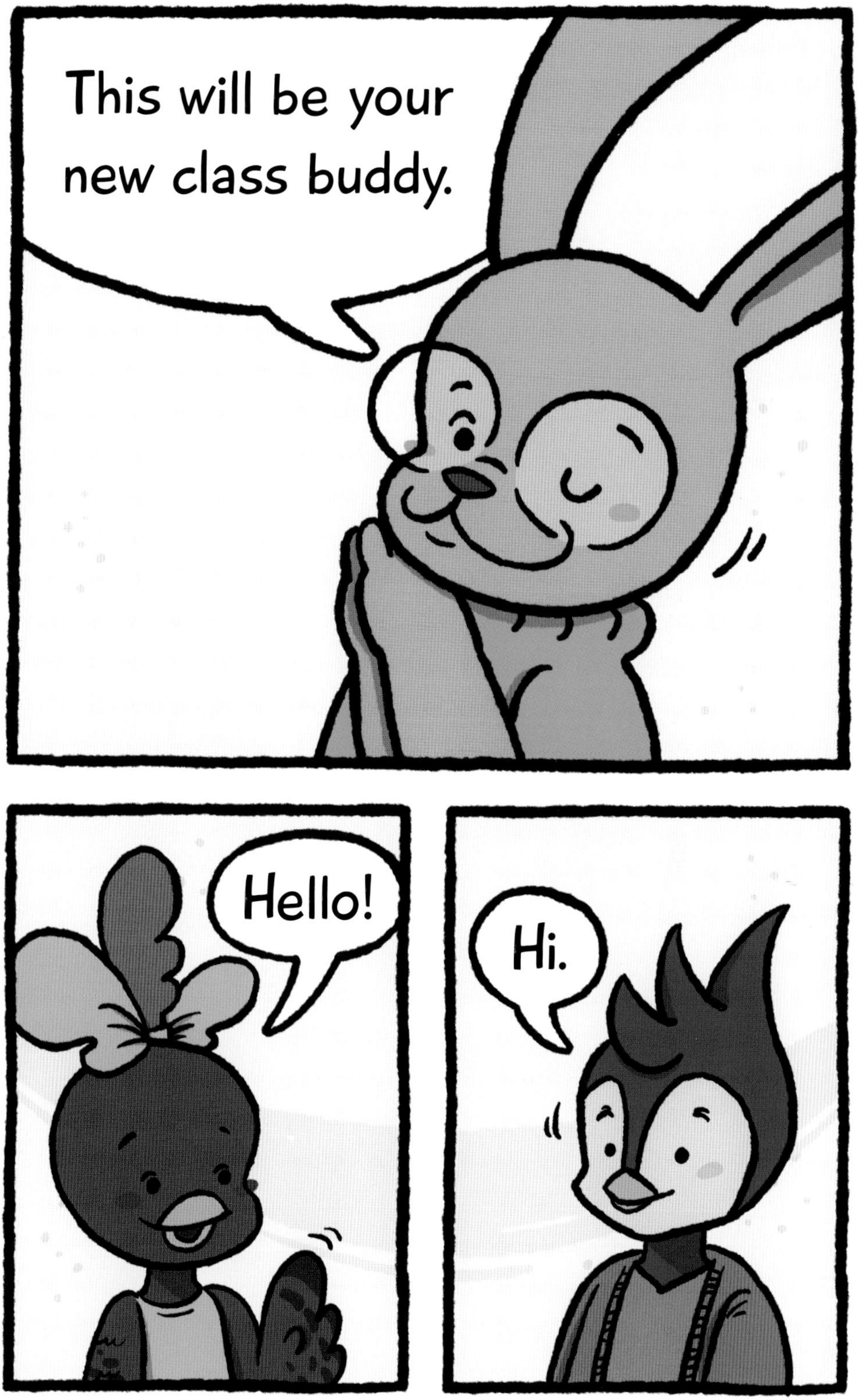
This will be your new class buddy.
Hello!
Hi.

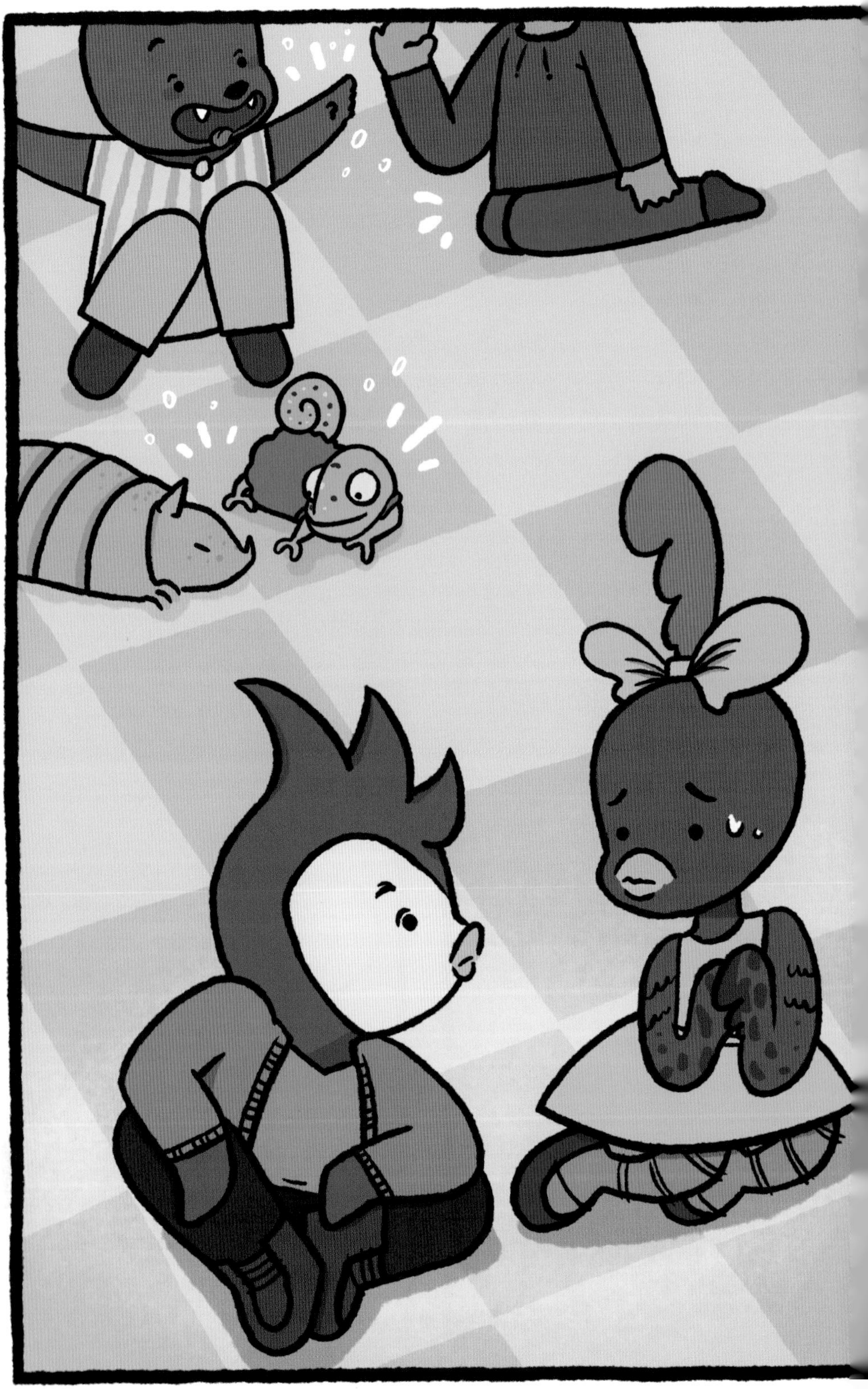

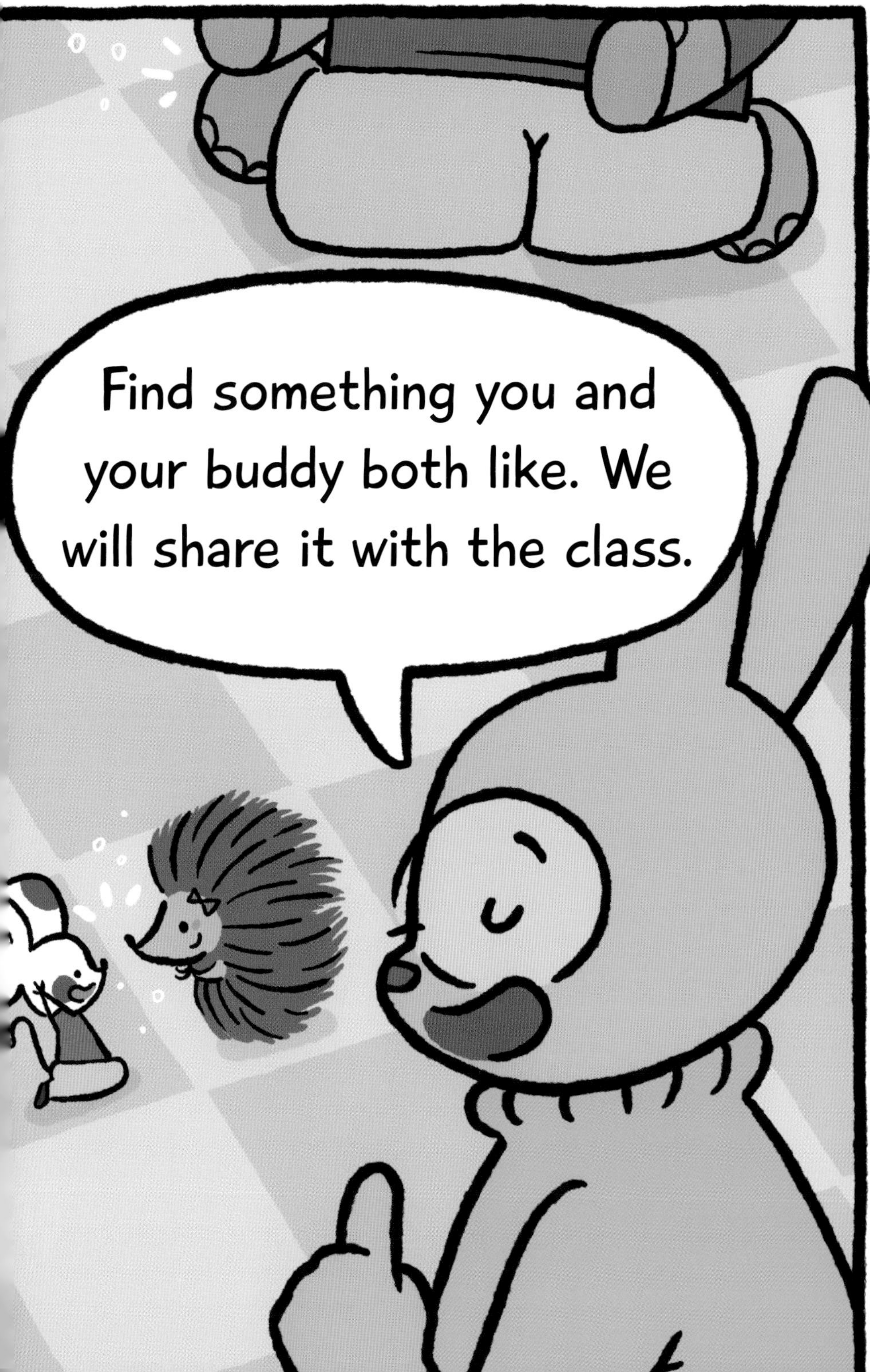
Find something you and your buddy both like. We will share it with the class.

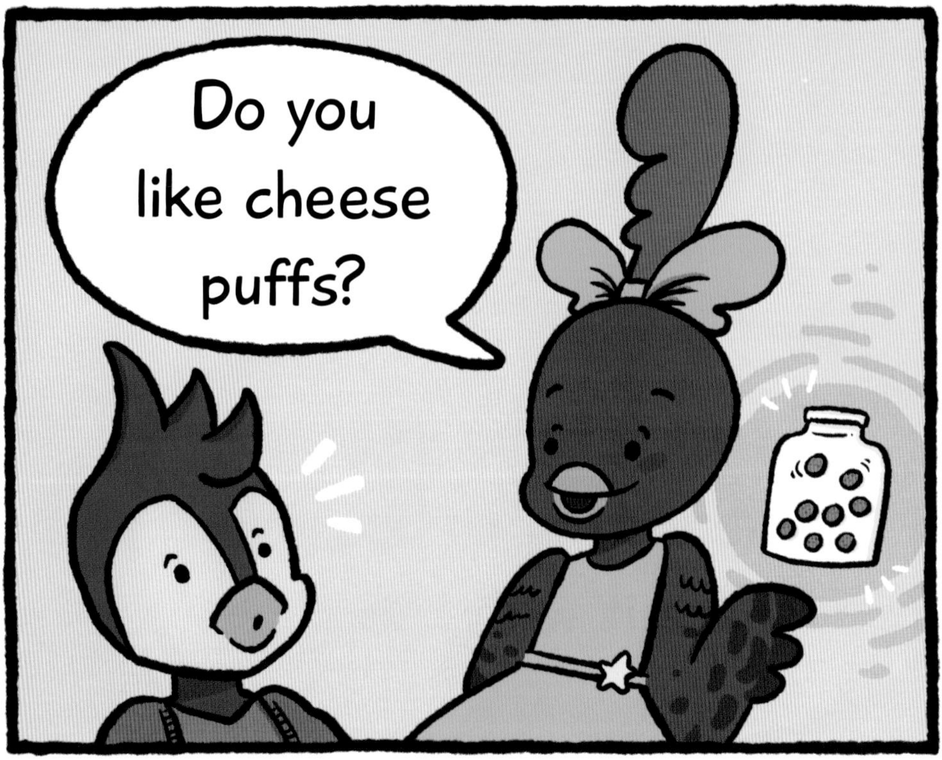
Do you like cheese puffs?

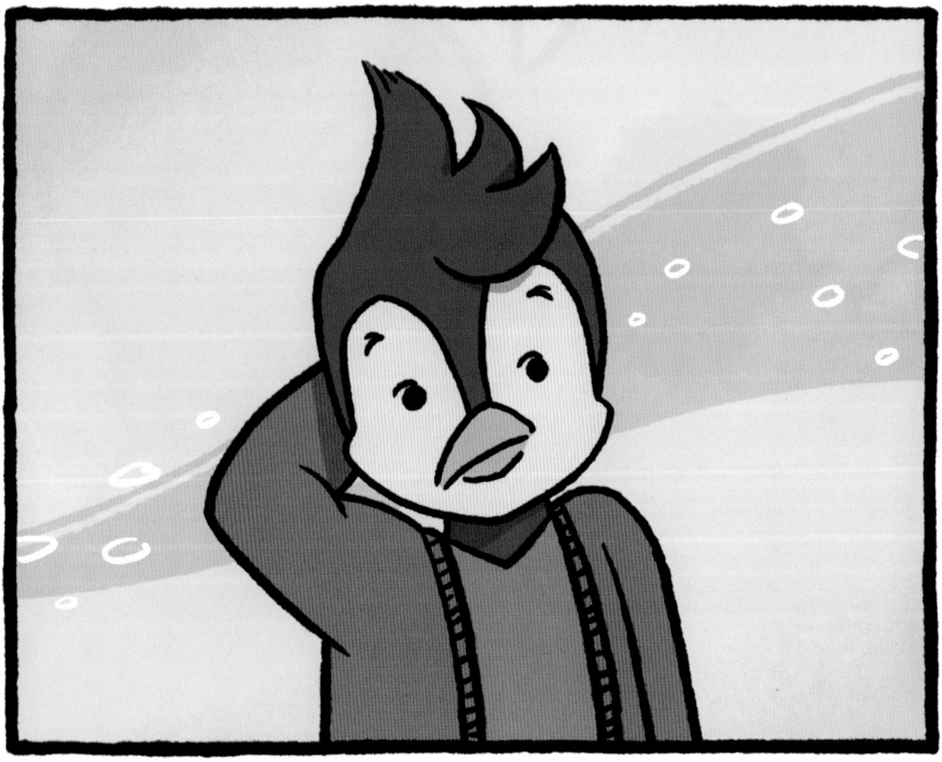

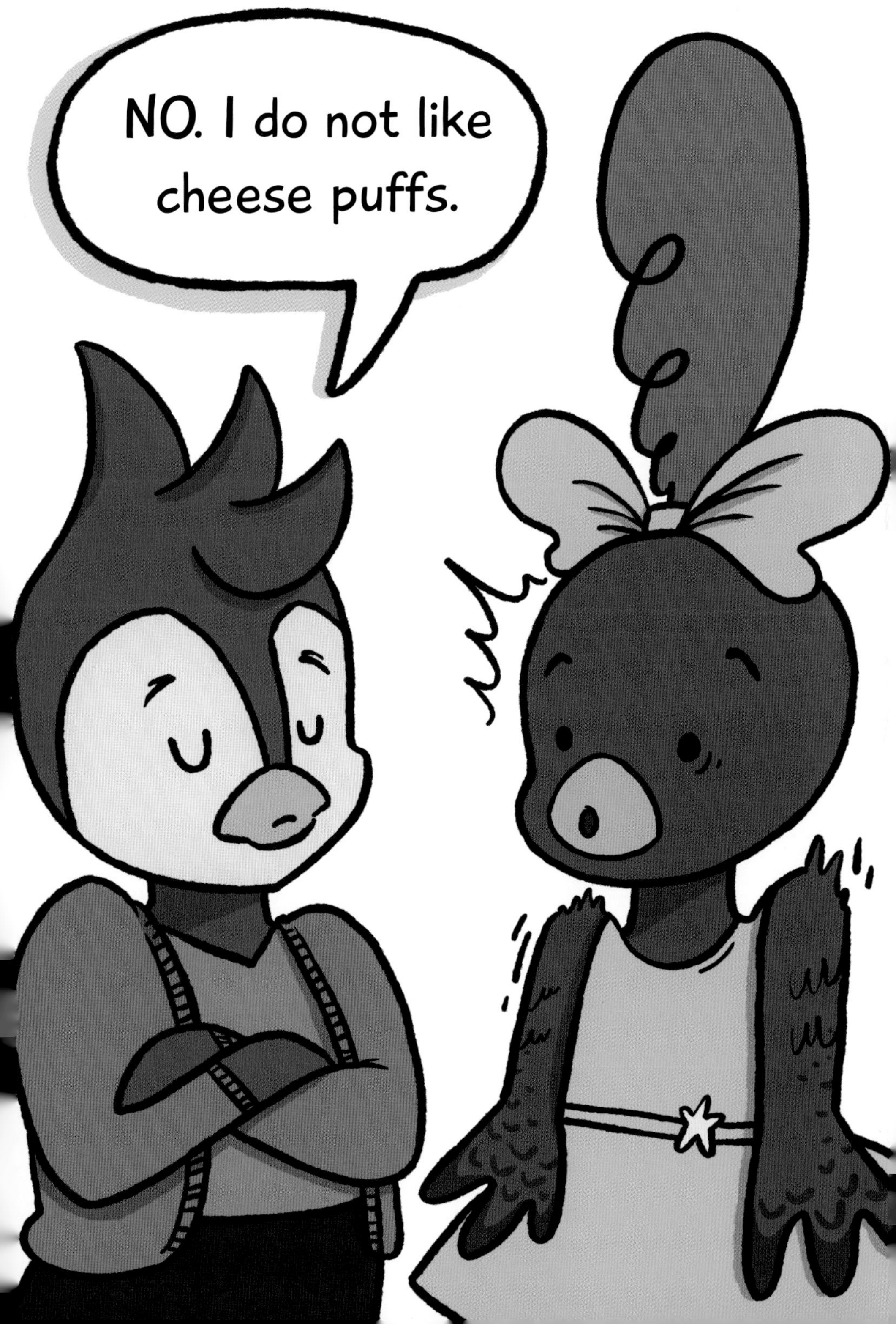
NO. I do not like cheese puffs.

This might be difficult.

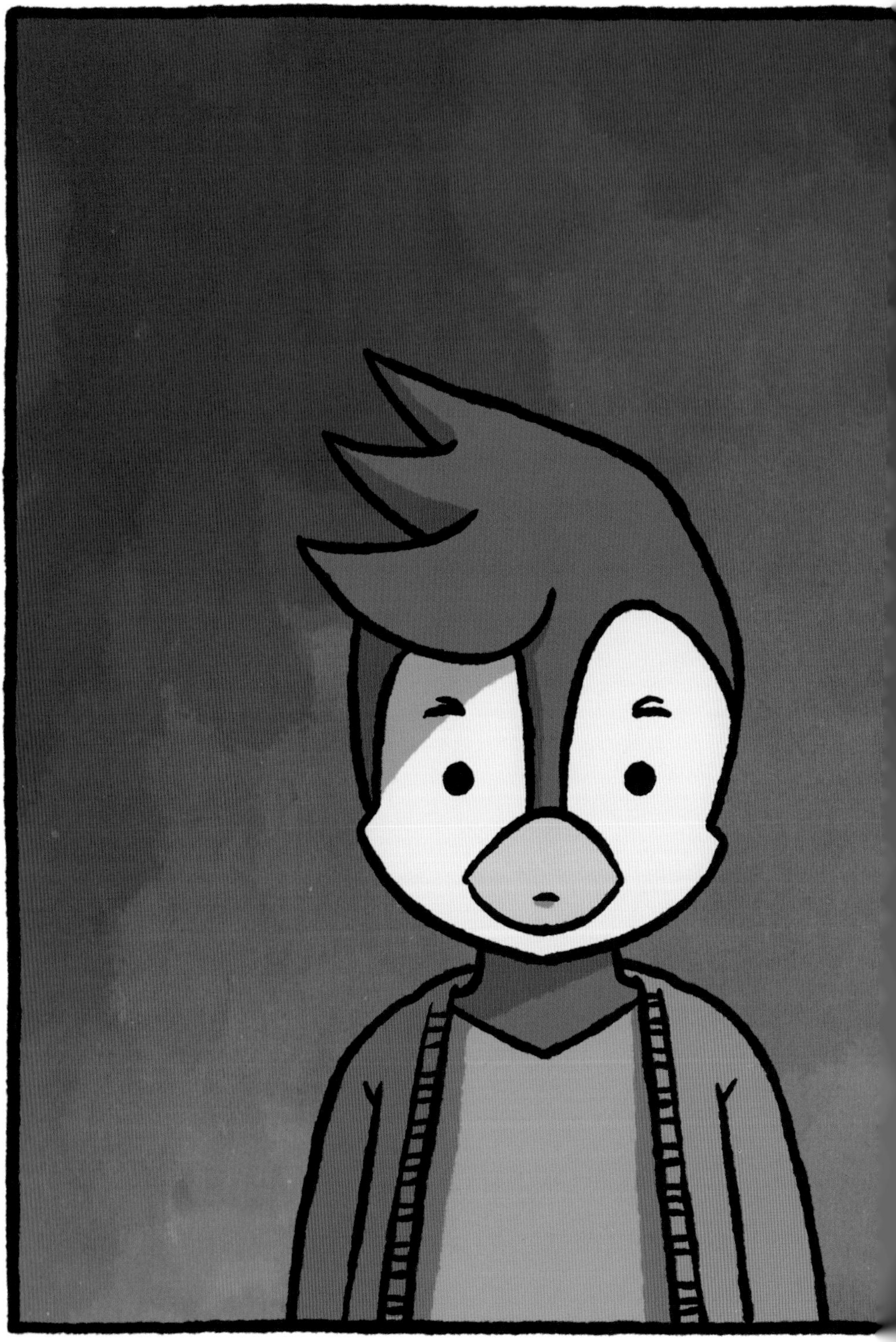

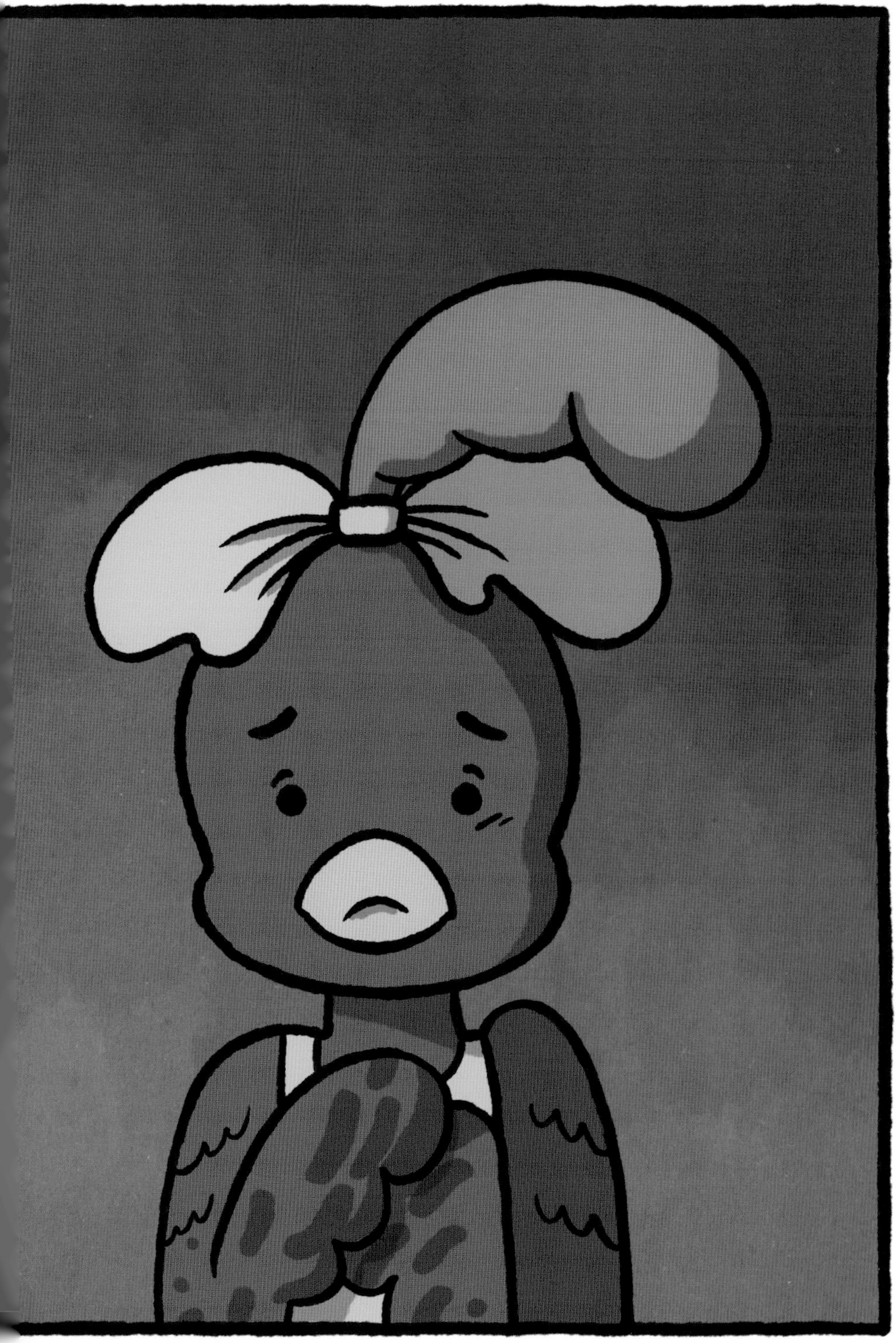

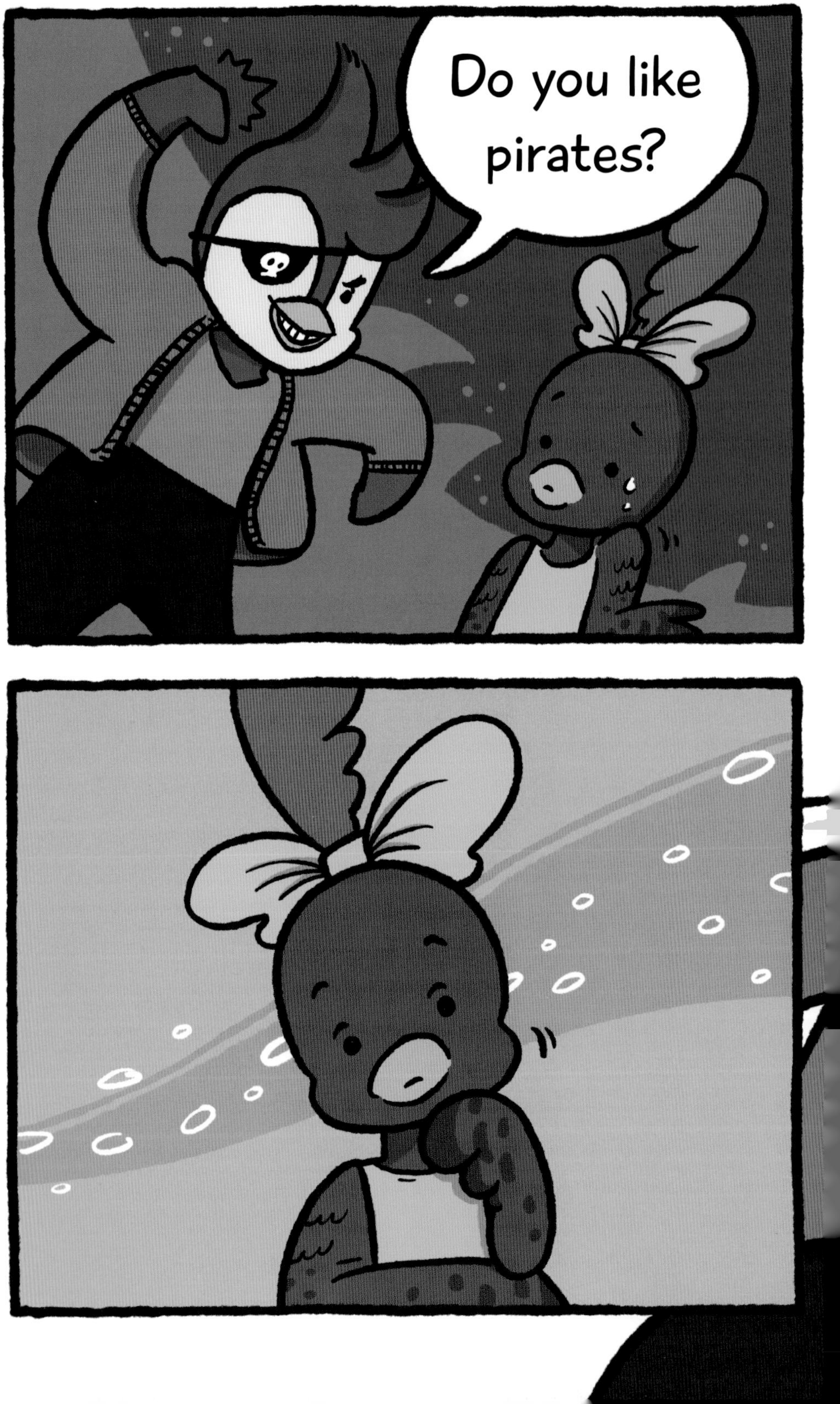
Do you like pirates?

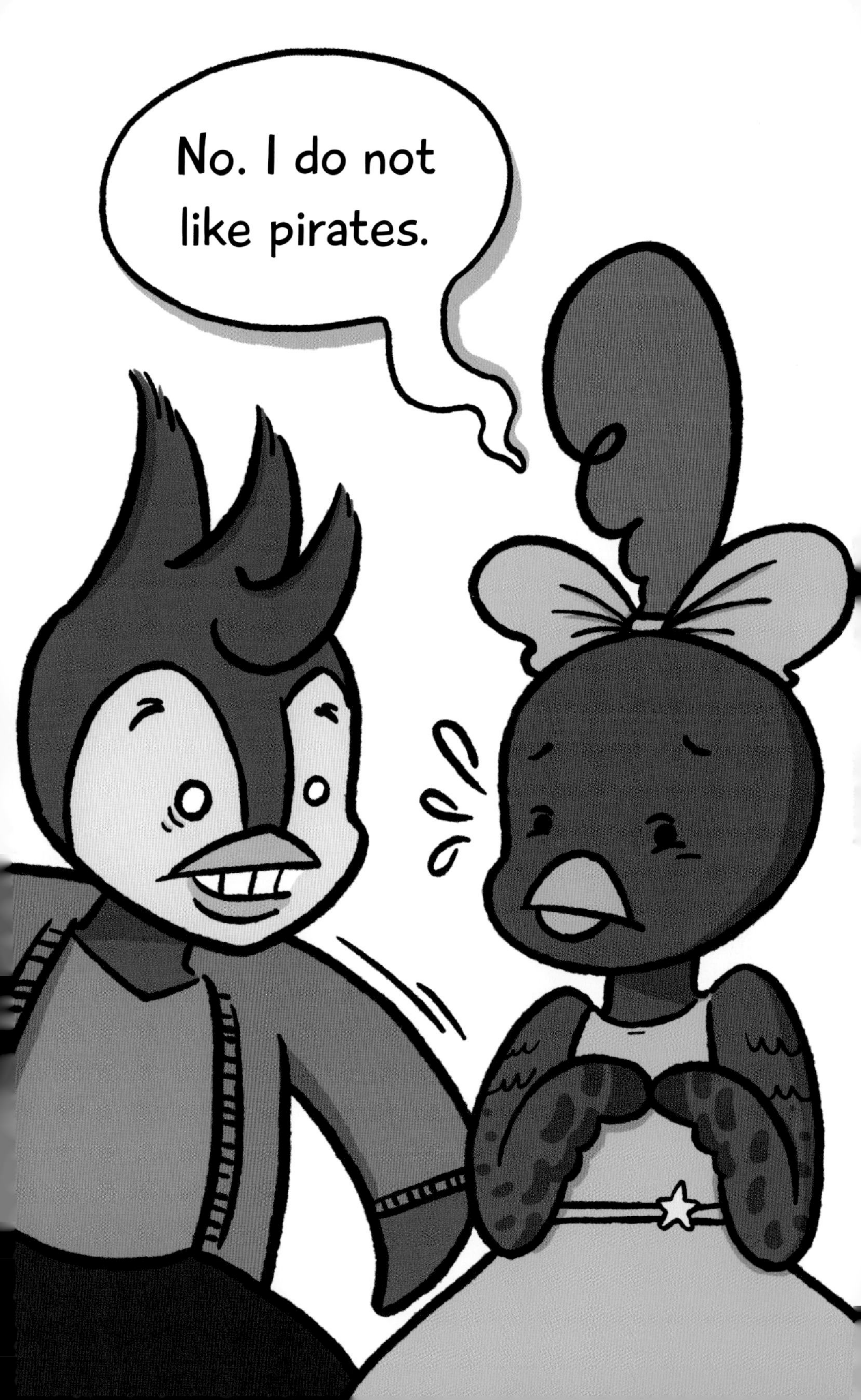
No. I do not like pirates.

This may even be...IMPOSSIBLE.

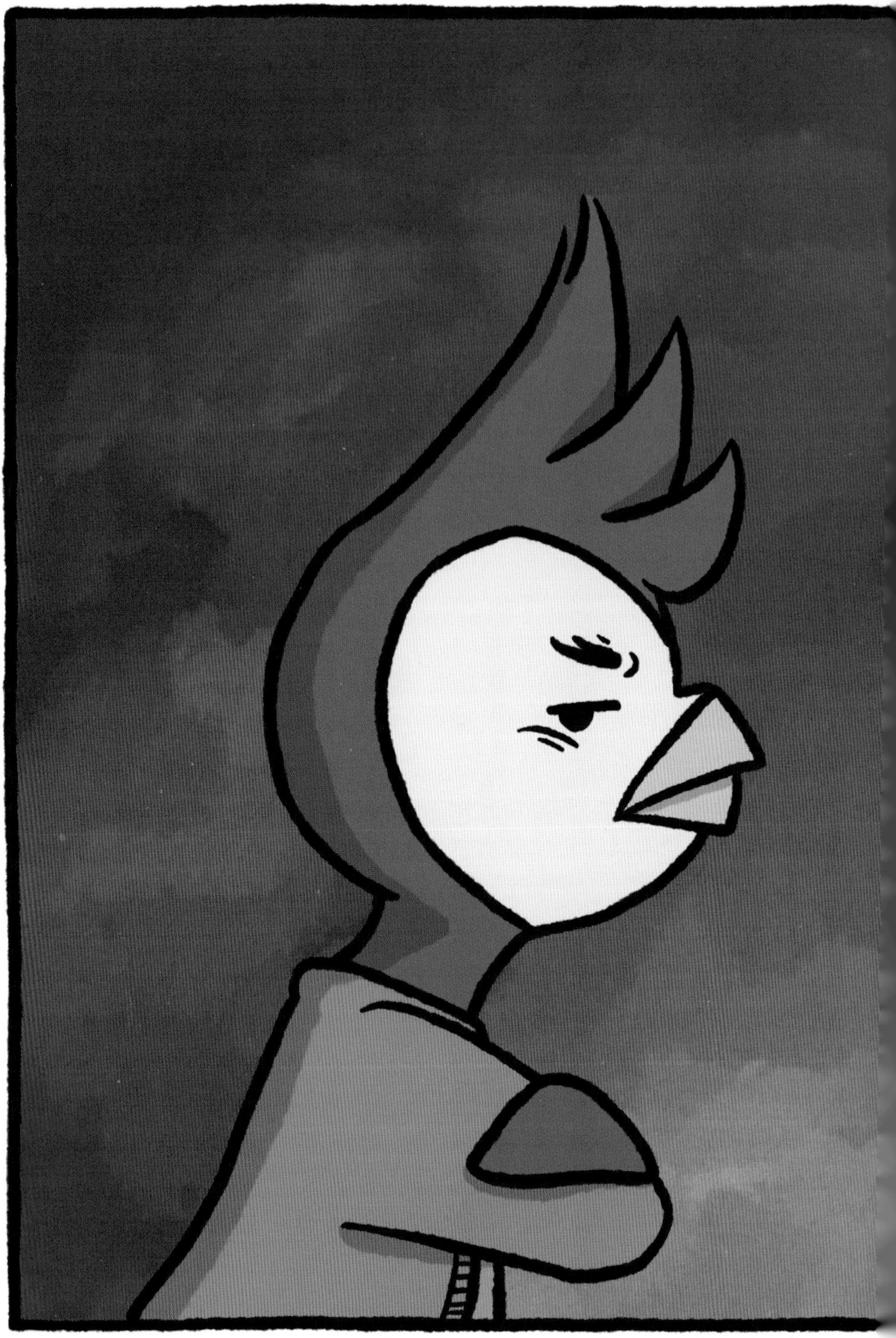

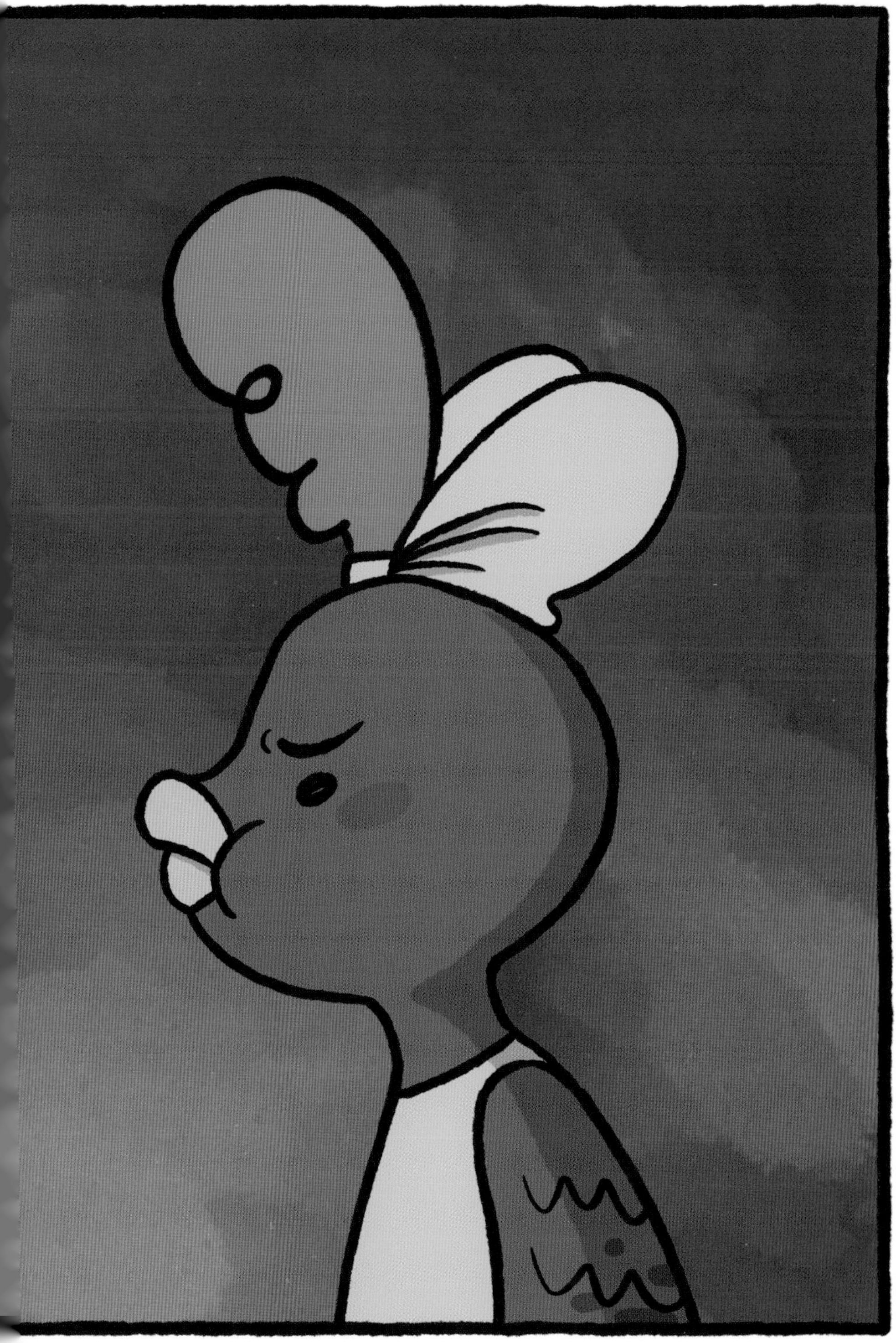

Chi-Chi and Pey-Pey talk for one full minute.

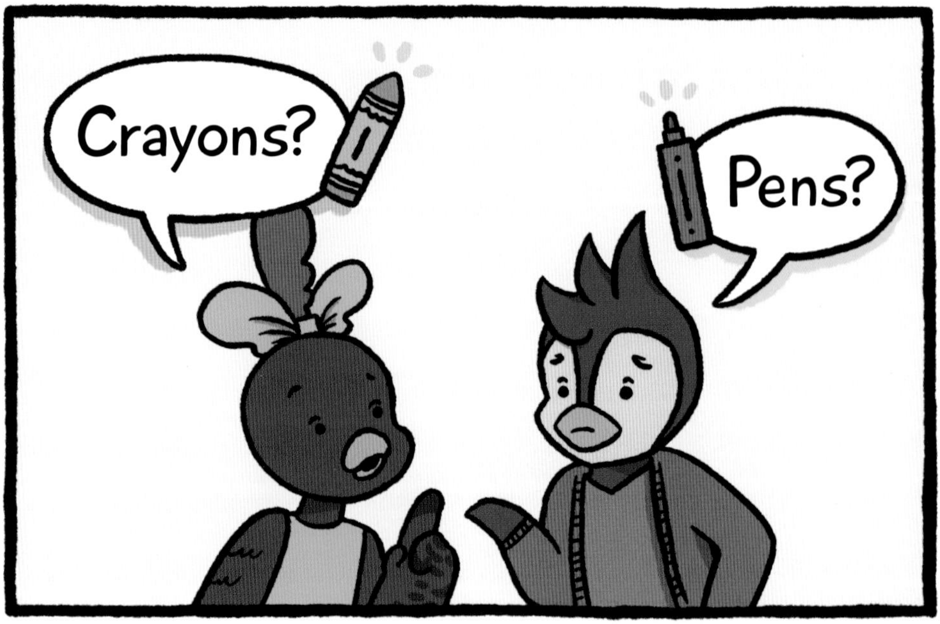
Crayons?
Pens?

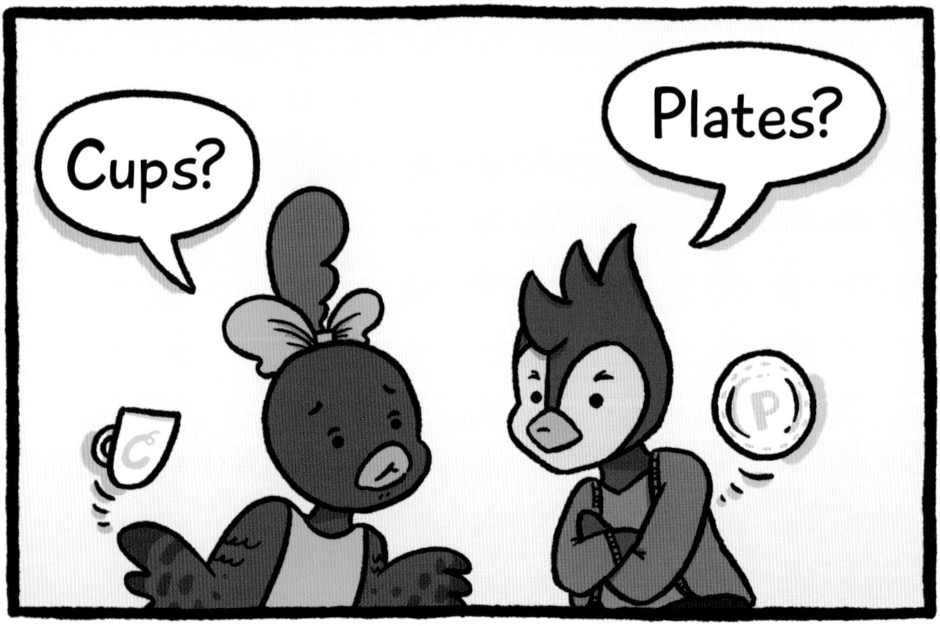
Cups?
Plates?

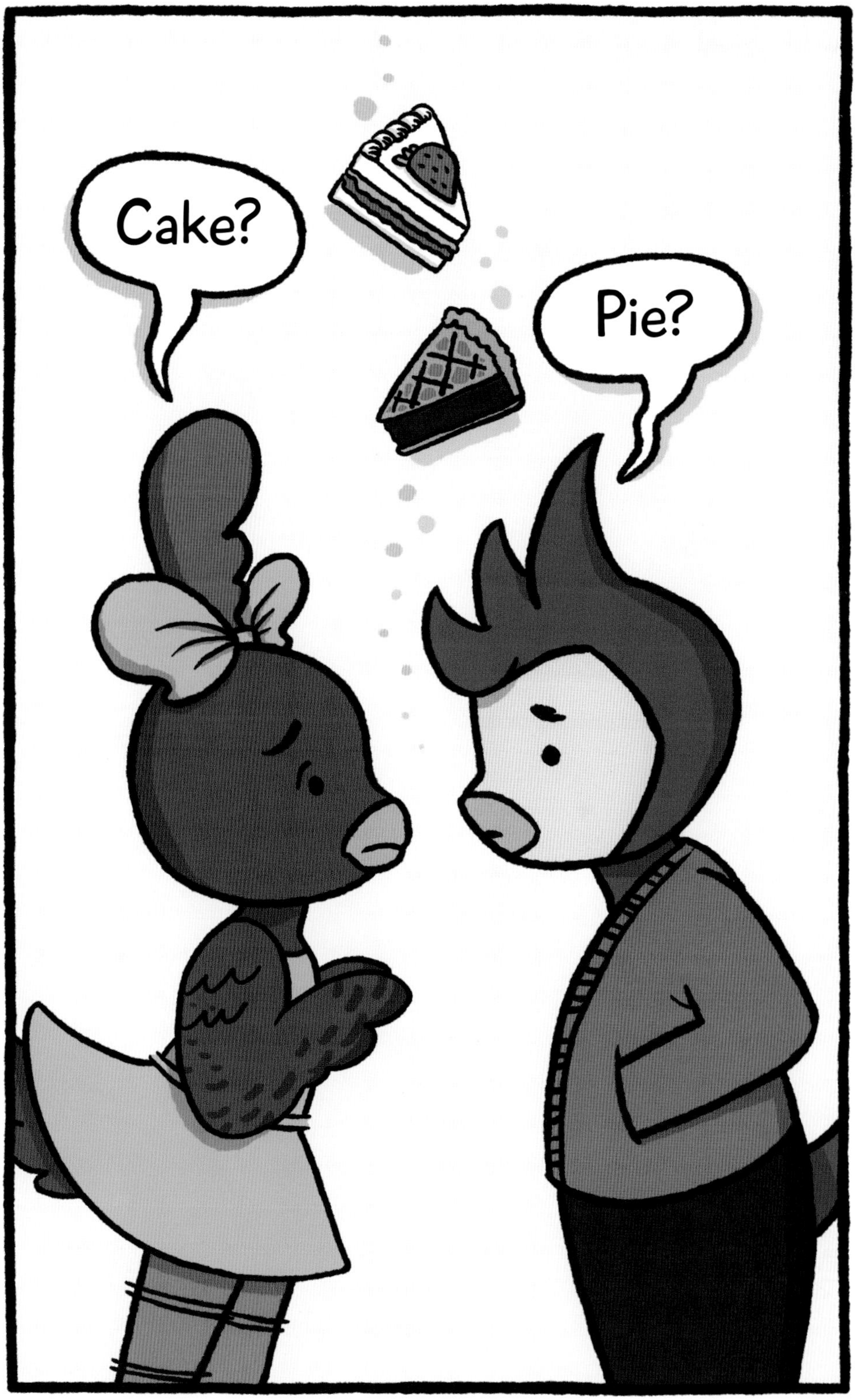
Cake?
Pie?

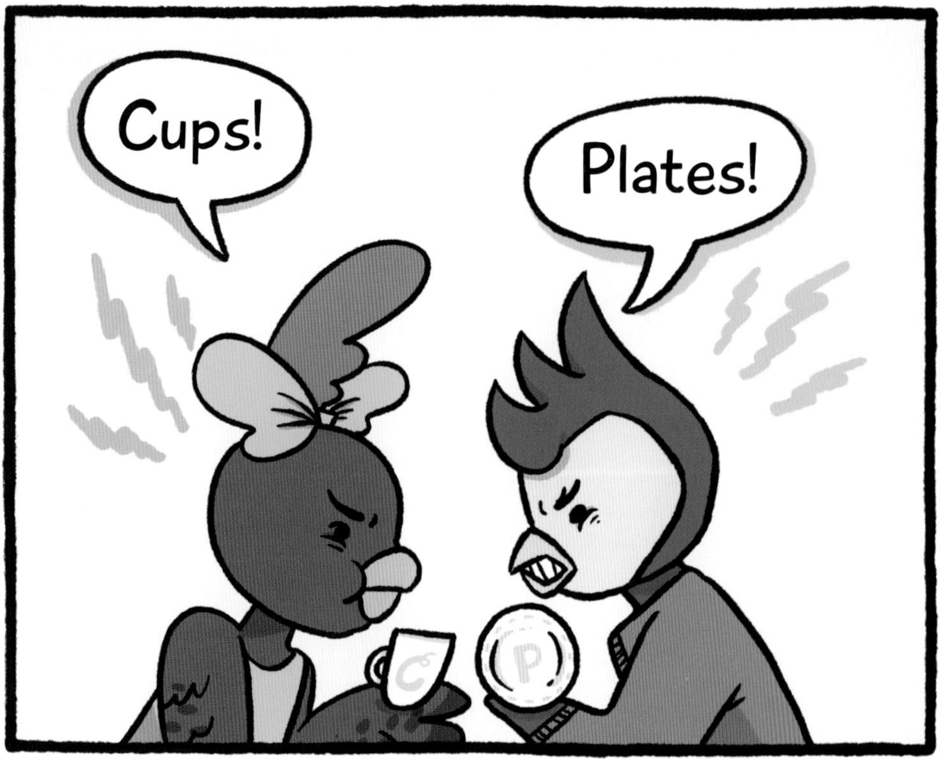
Cups!
Plates!

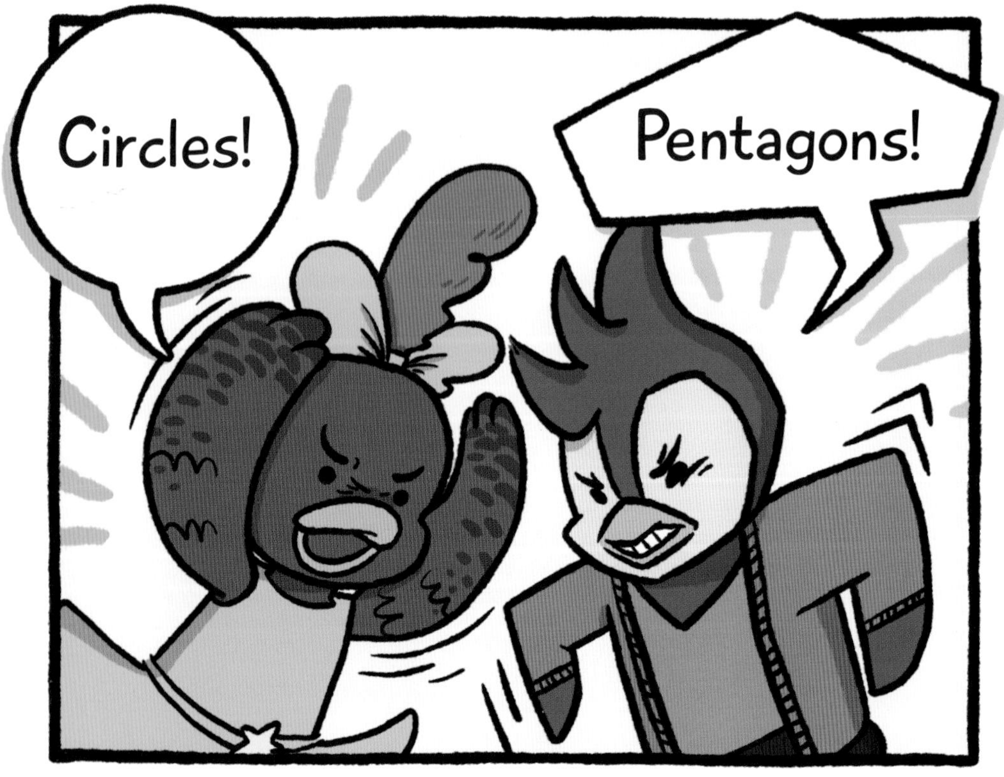
Circles!
Pentagons!

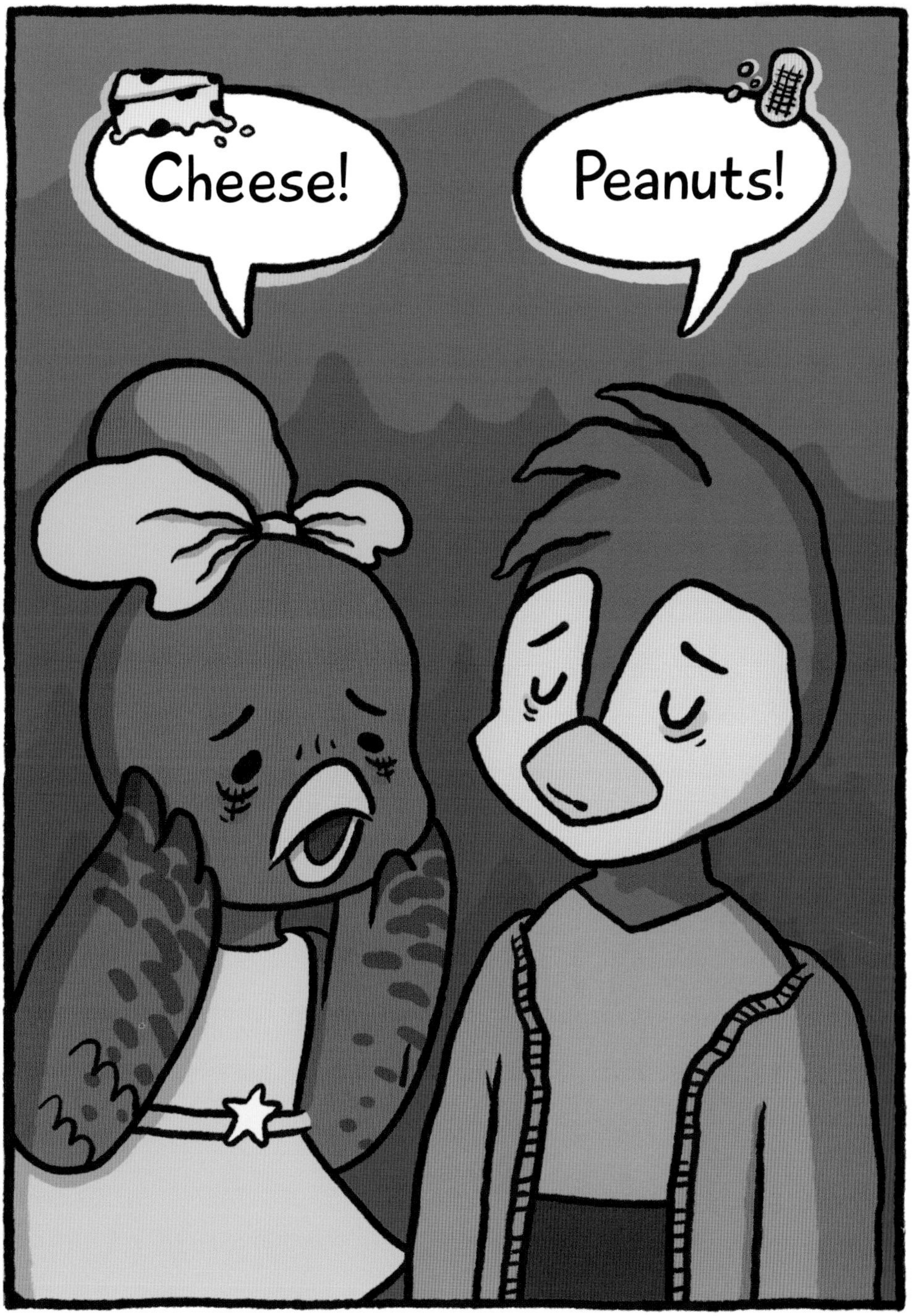
Cheese!
Peanuts!

They do not have a single thing in common.

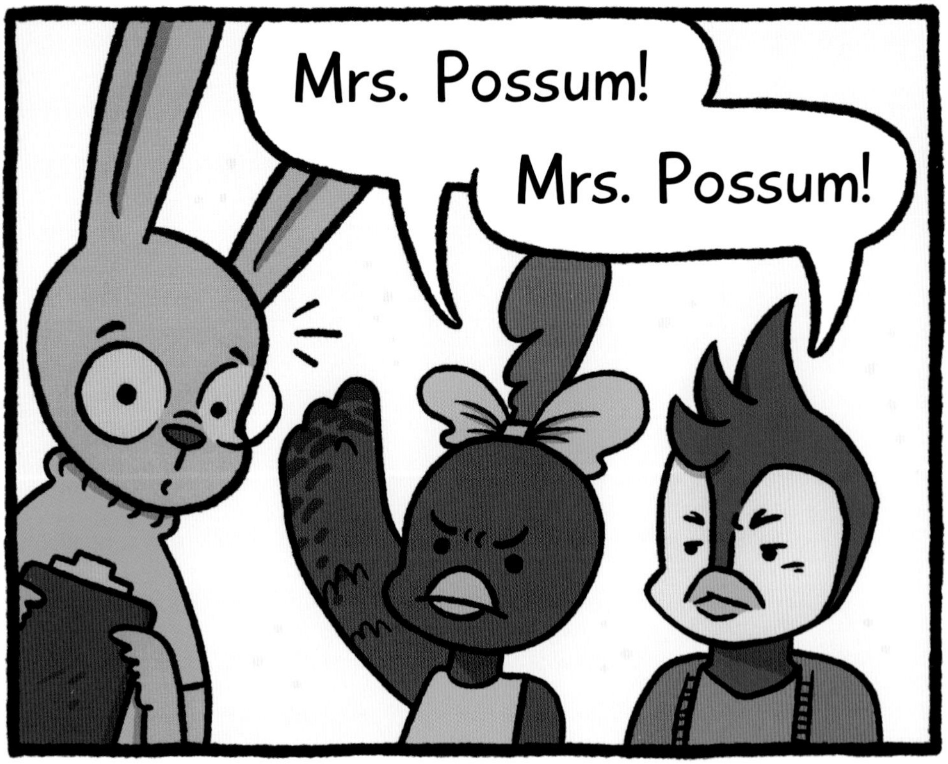
Mrs. Possum!
Mrs. Possum!

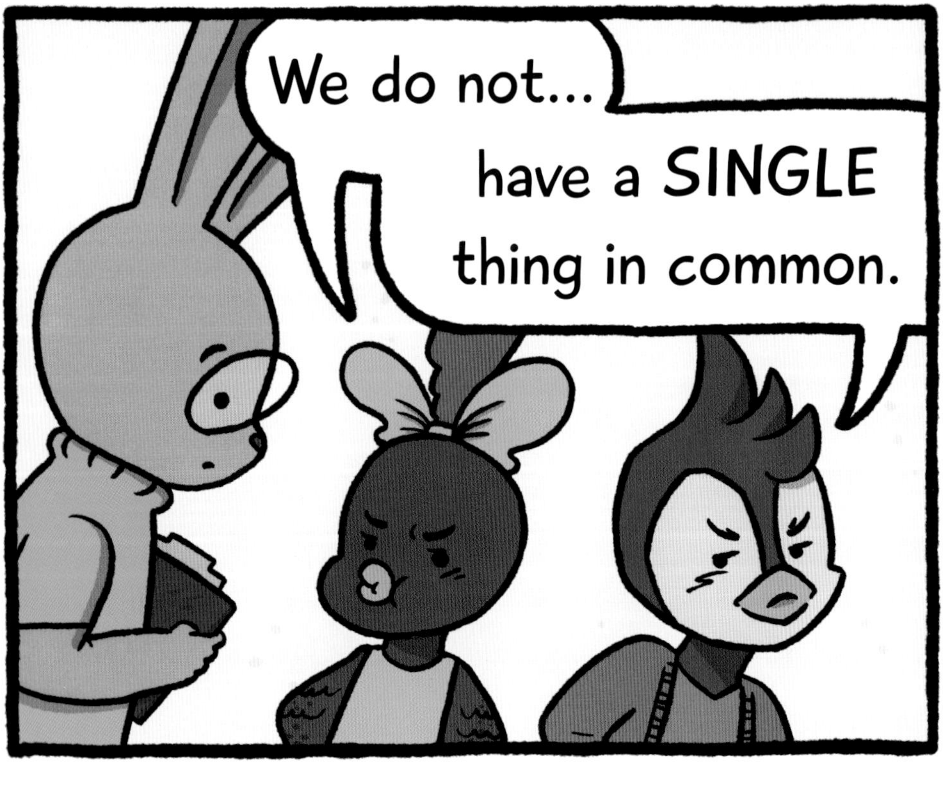
We do not...
have a SINGLE thing in common.

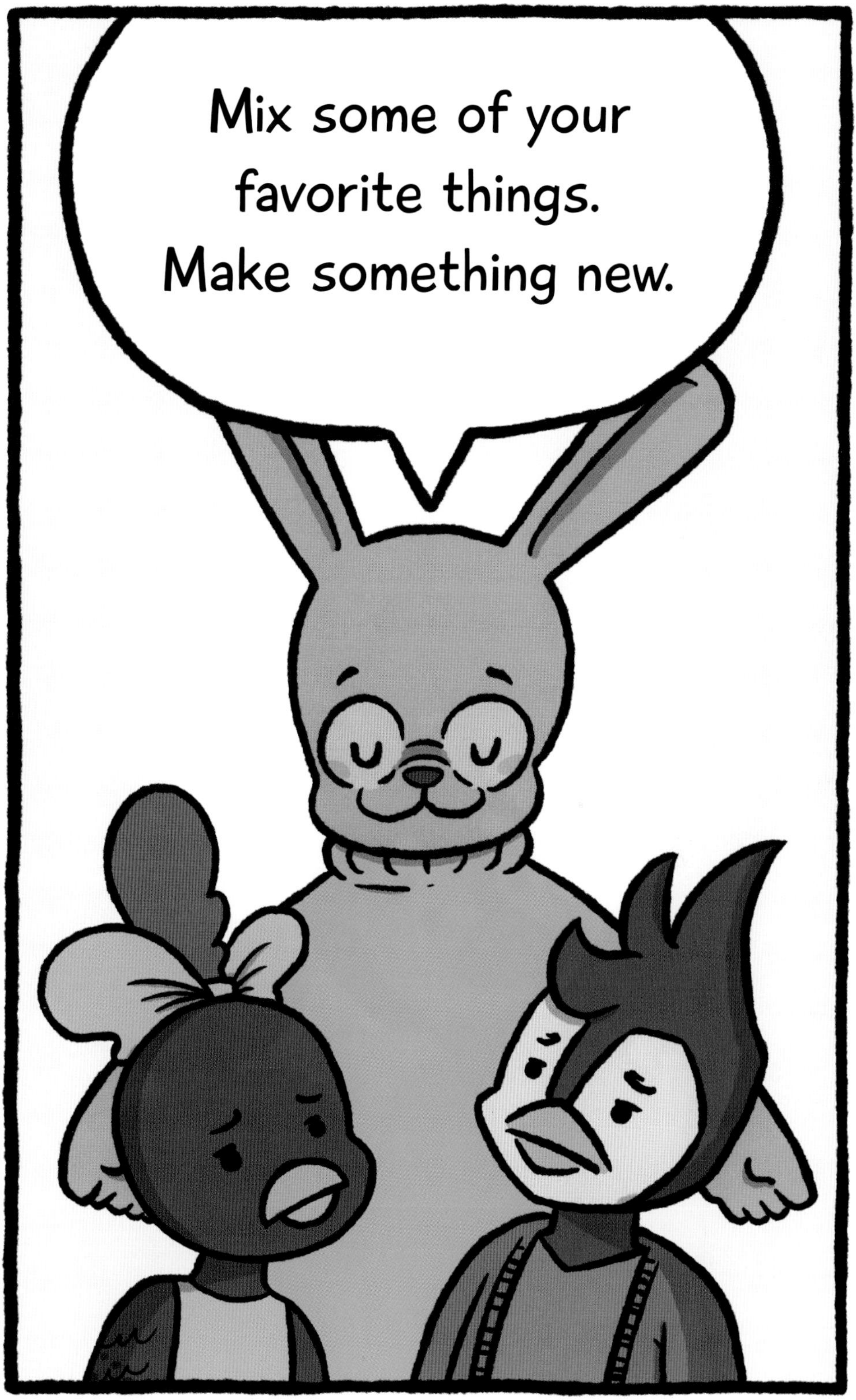
Mix some of your favorite things. Make something new.

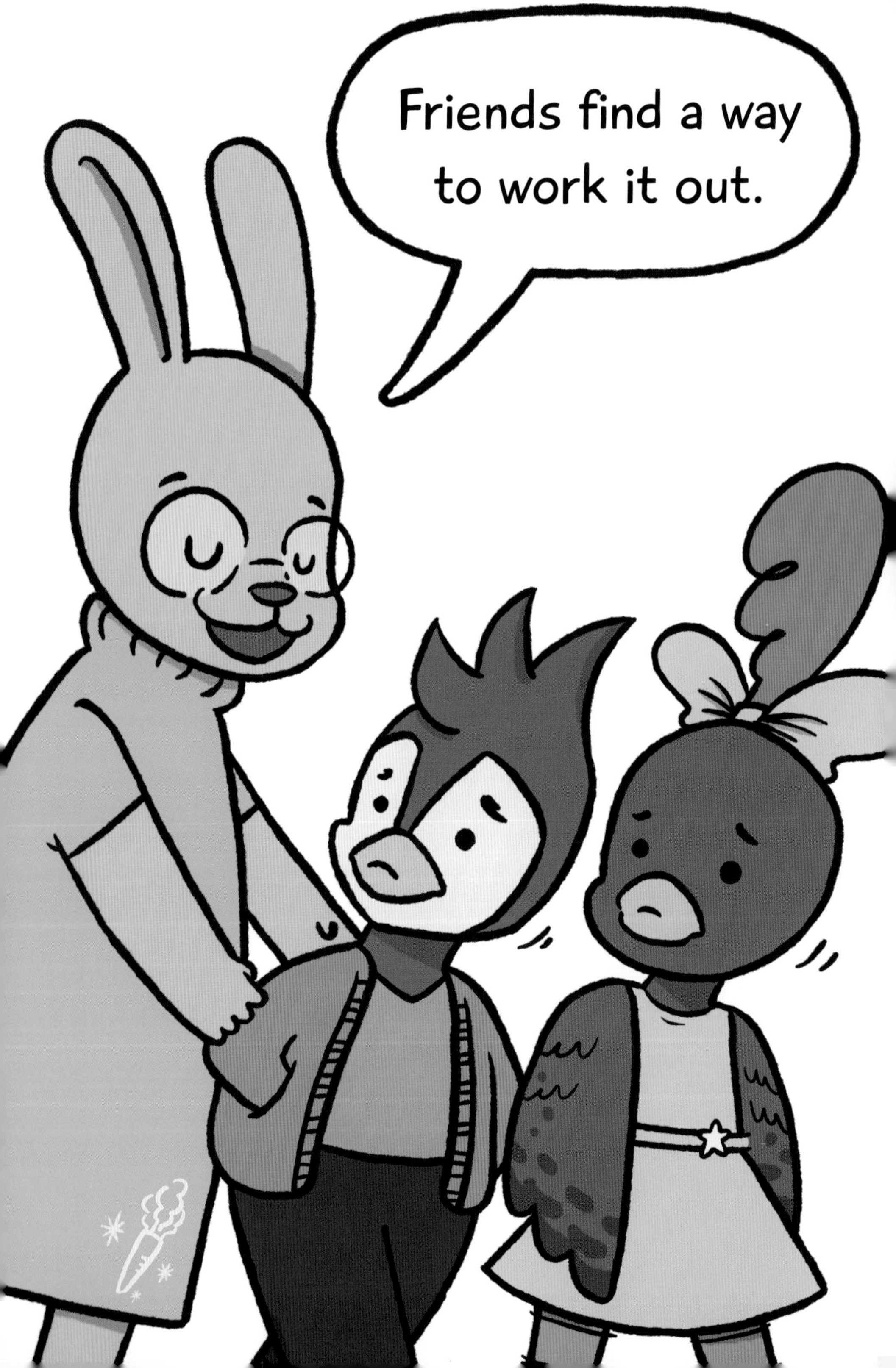
Friends find a way to work it out.

Pey-Pey looks at Chi-Chi.

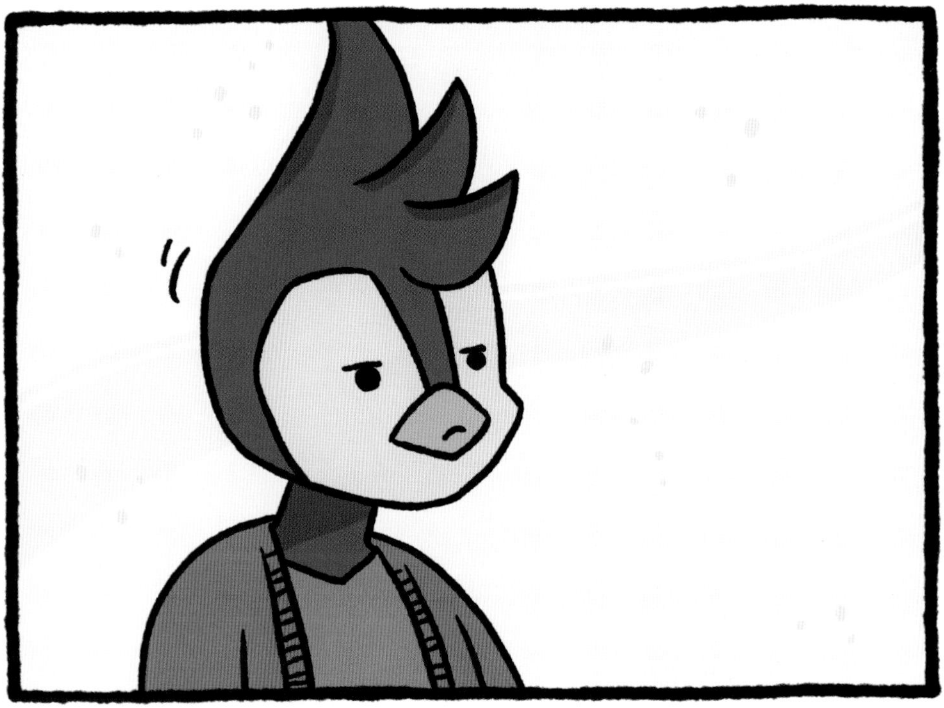

Chi-Chi looks at Pey-Pey.

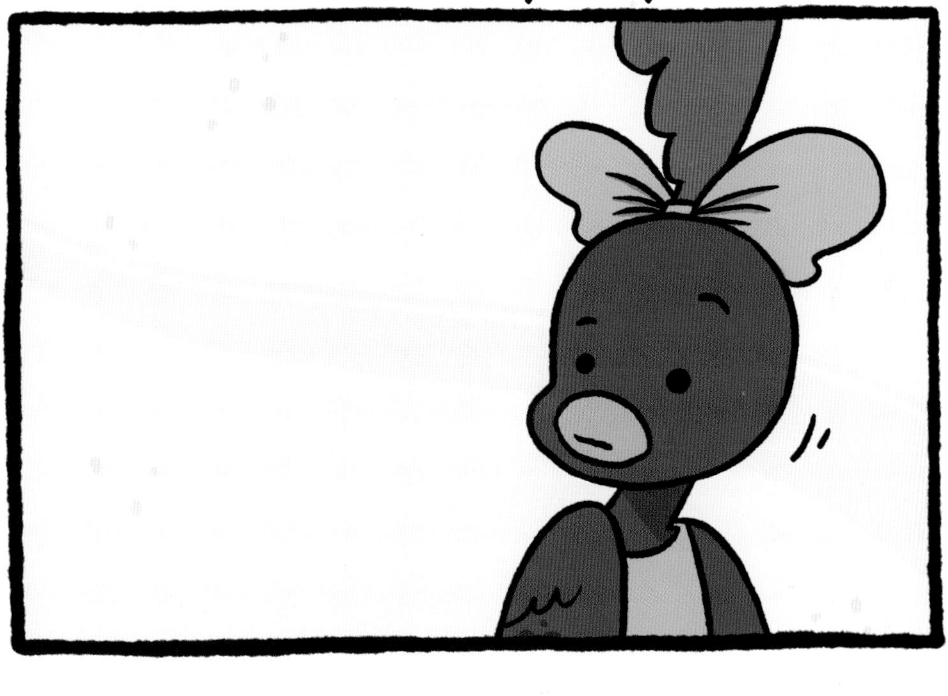

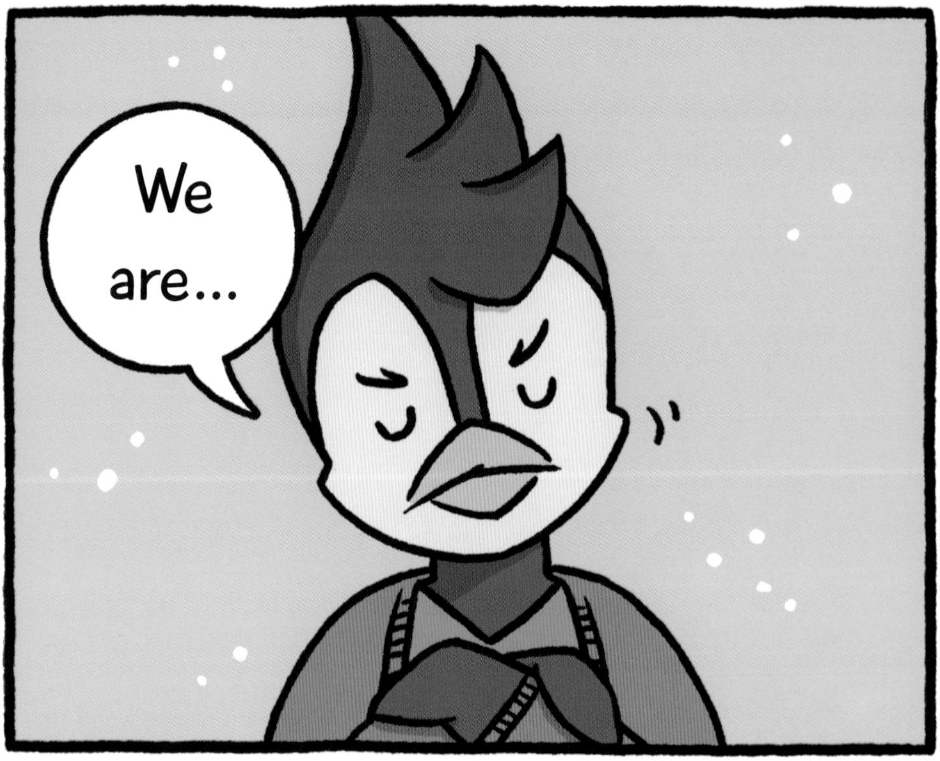
We are...

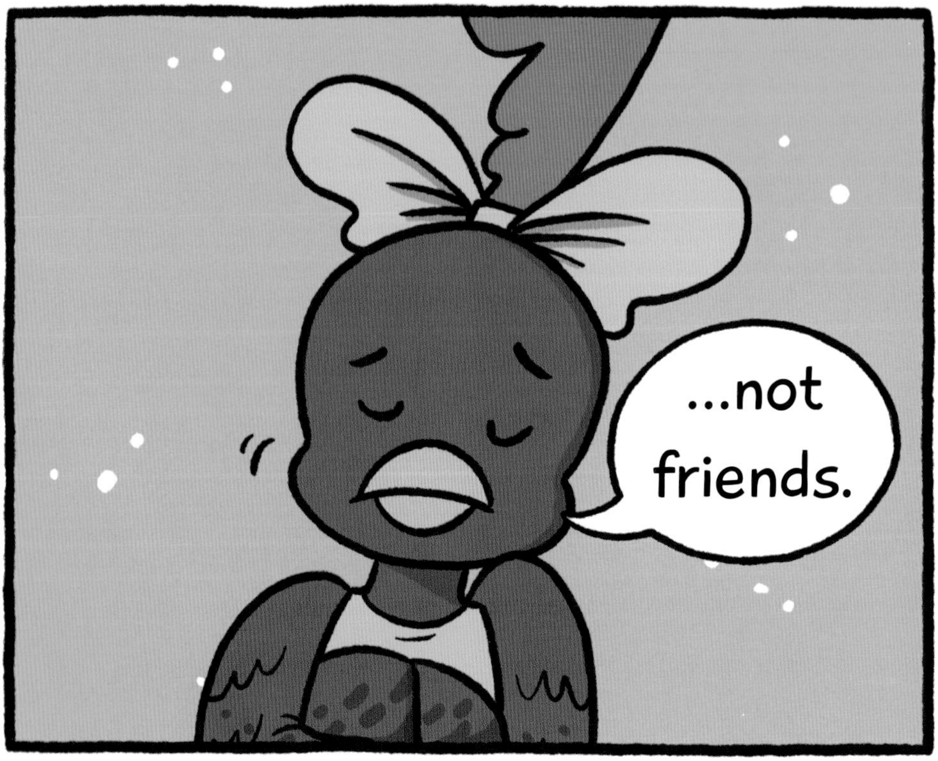
...not friends.

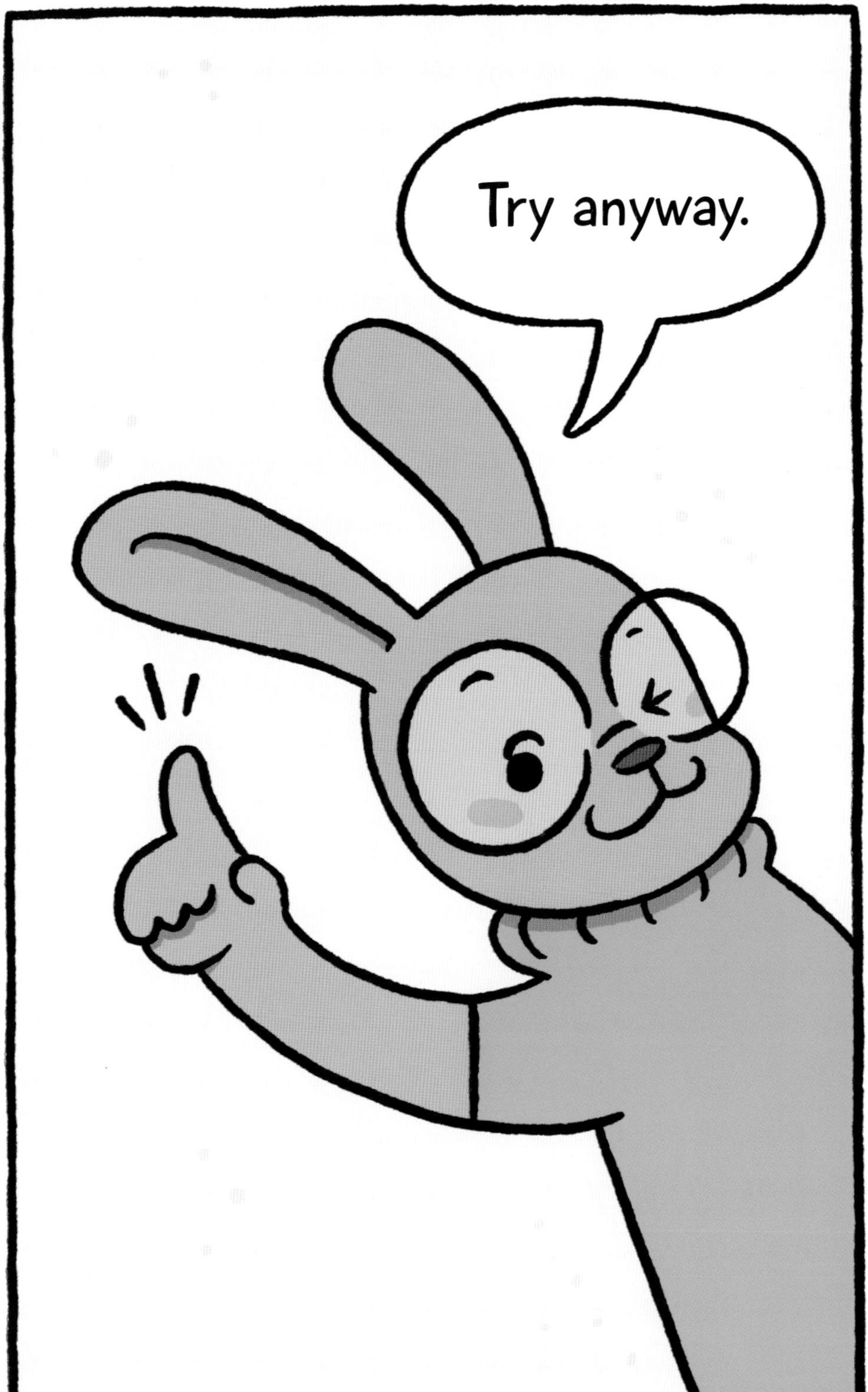
Try anyway.

Chi-Chi and Pey-Pey share their favorite snacks.

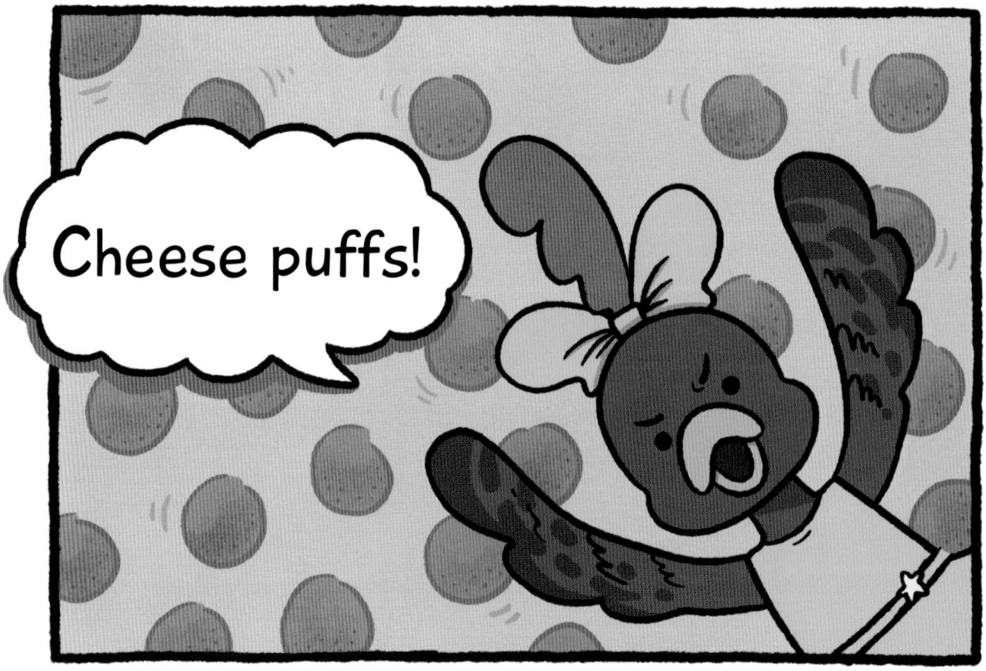
Cheese puffs!

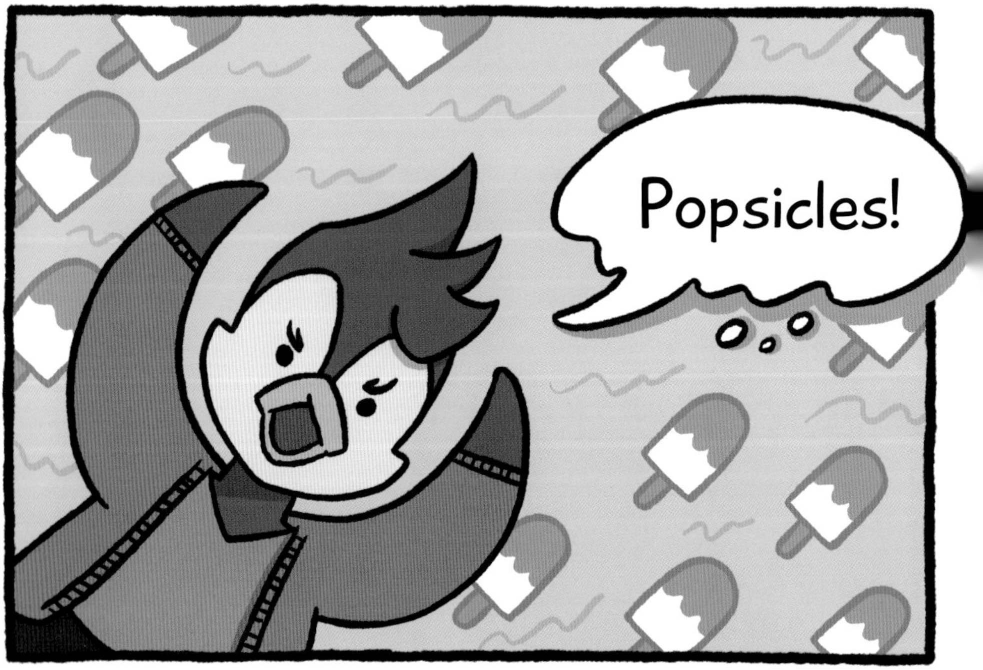
Popsicles!

Cheese-puff Popsicles are NOT yummy!

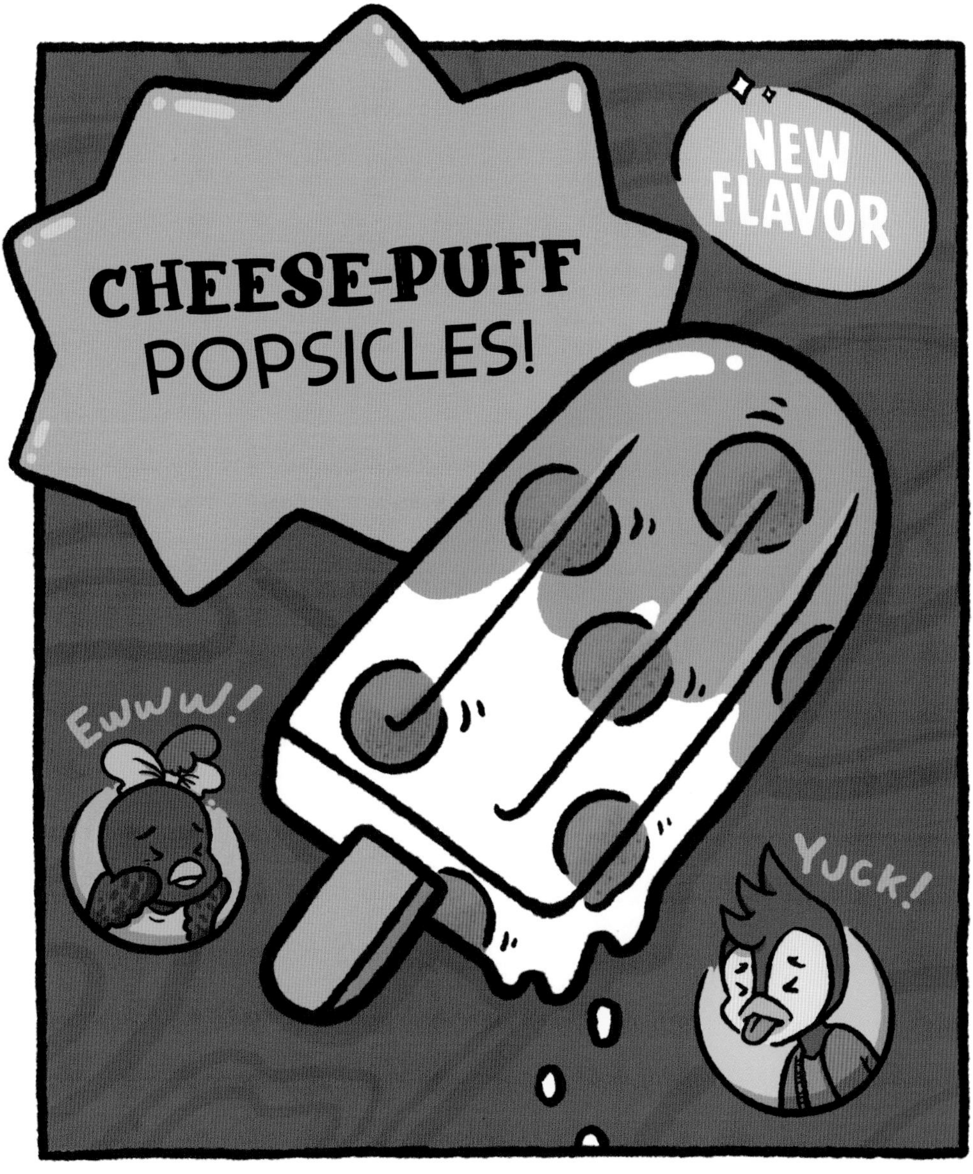
CHEESE-PUFF POPSICLES!
NEW FLAVOR
EWWW!
YUCK!

Chi-Chi and Pey-Pey share their favorite toys.

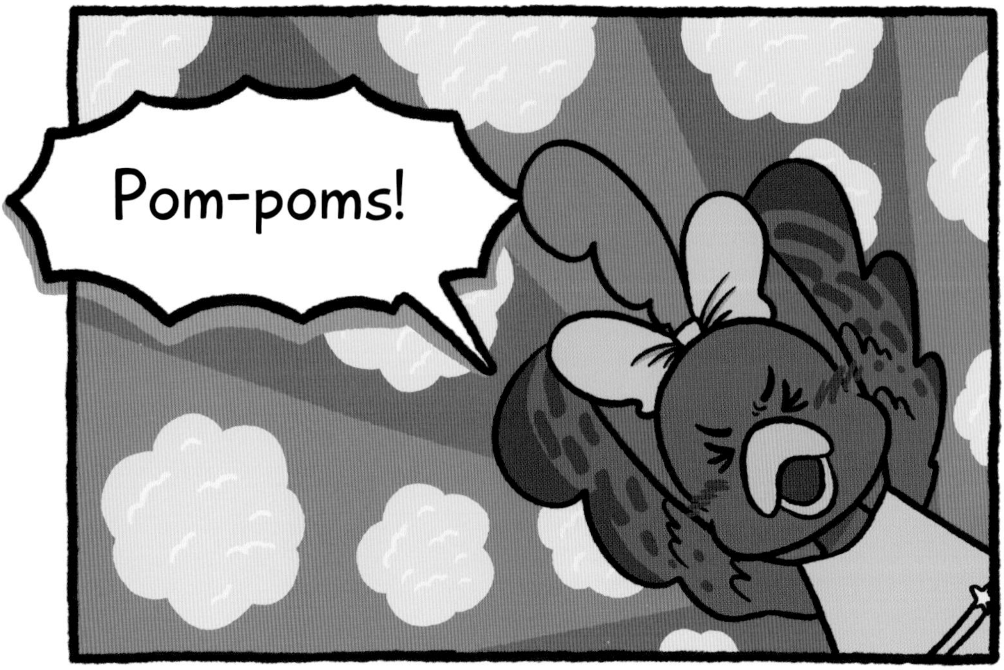
Pom-poms!

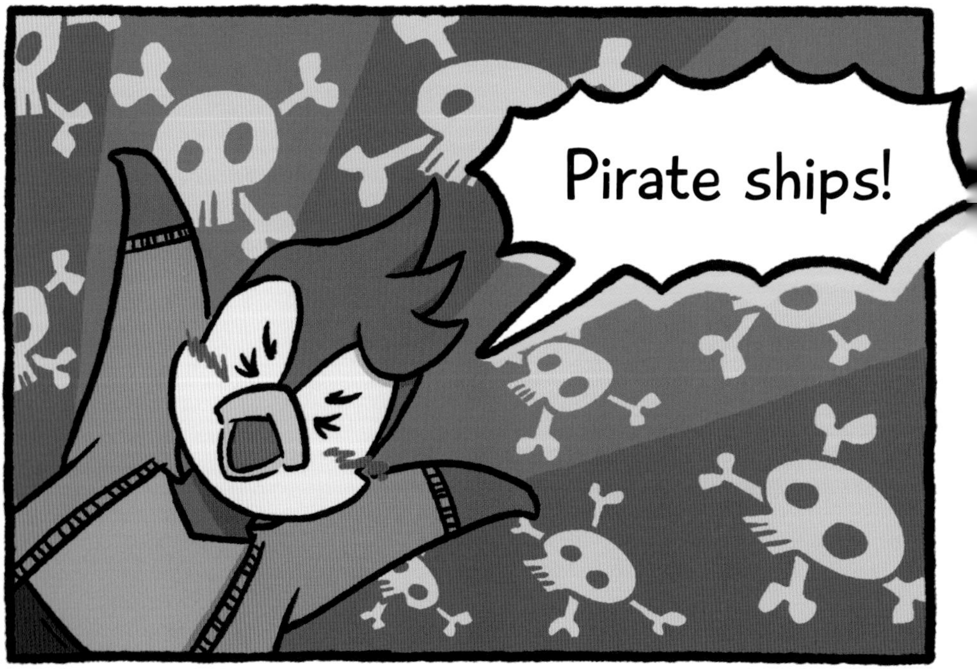
Pirate ships!

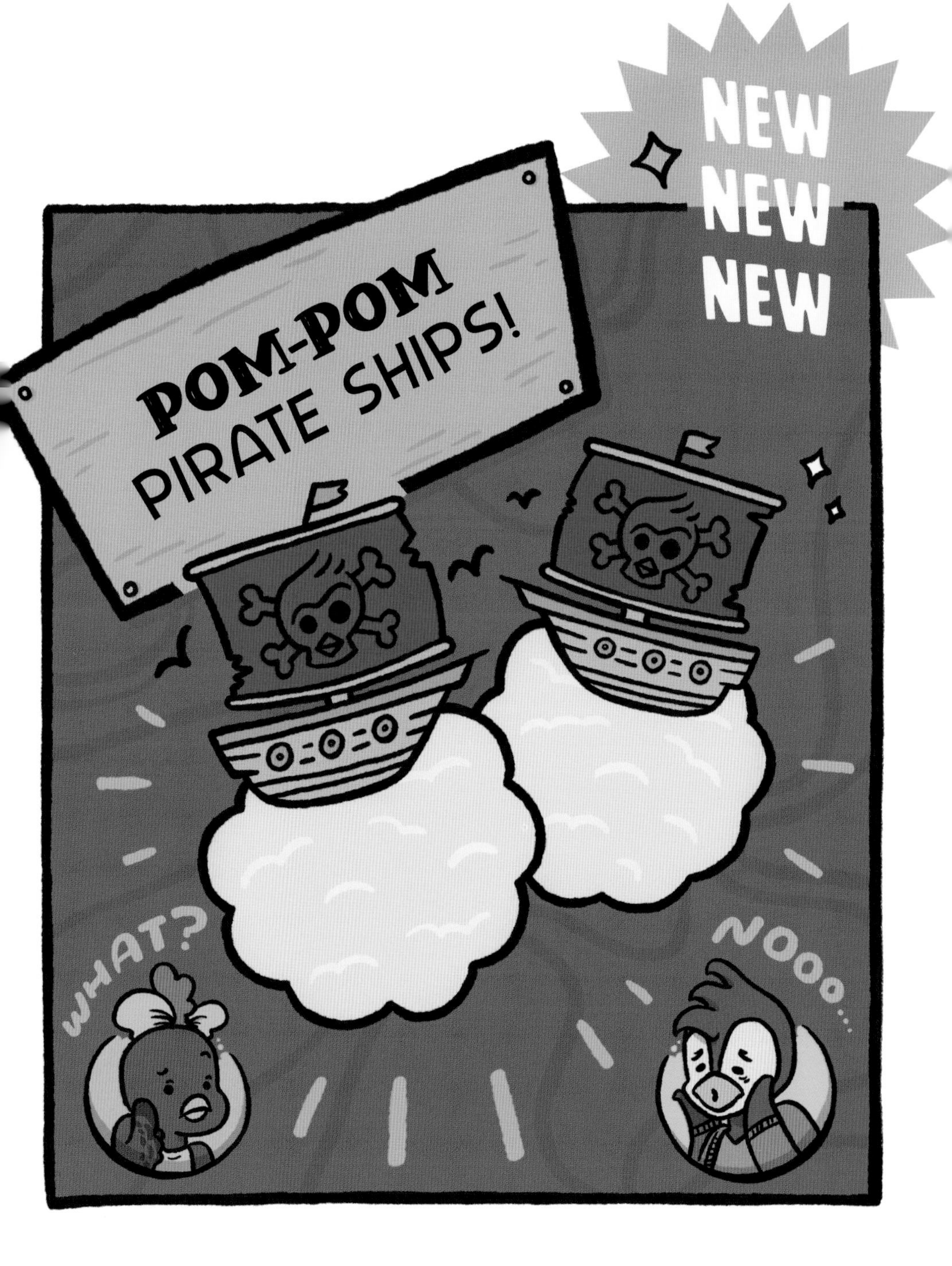
NEW
NEW
NEW
POM-POM
PIRATE SHIPS!
WHAT?
NOOO...

Pirate ships and pom-poms do NOT go together.

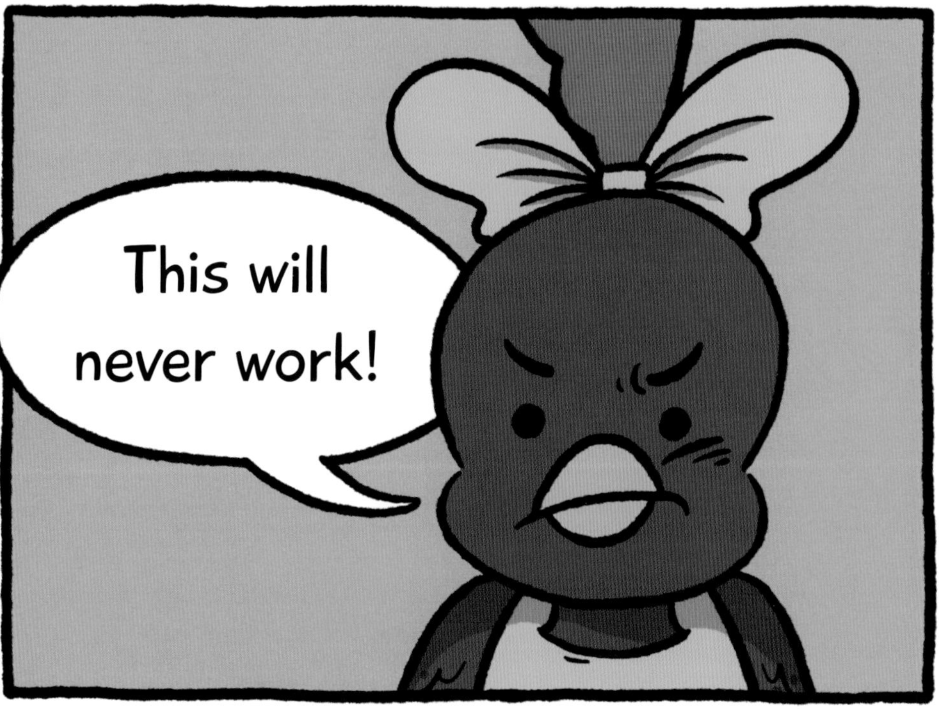
This will never work!

Chi-Chi dances away.

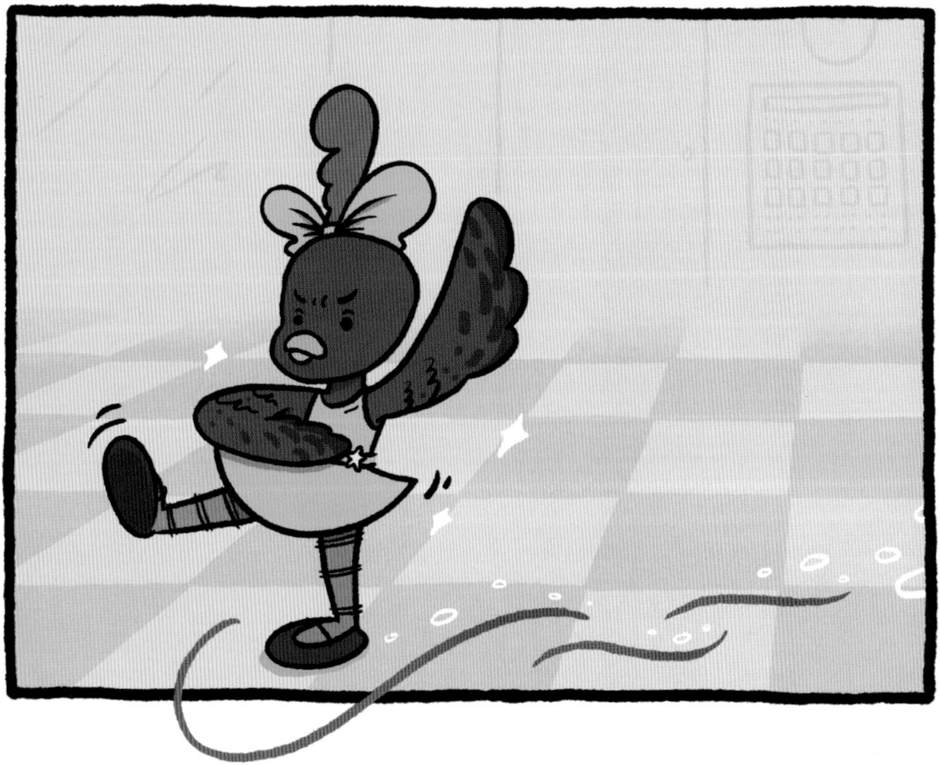

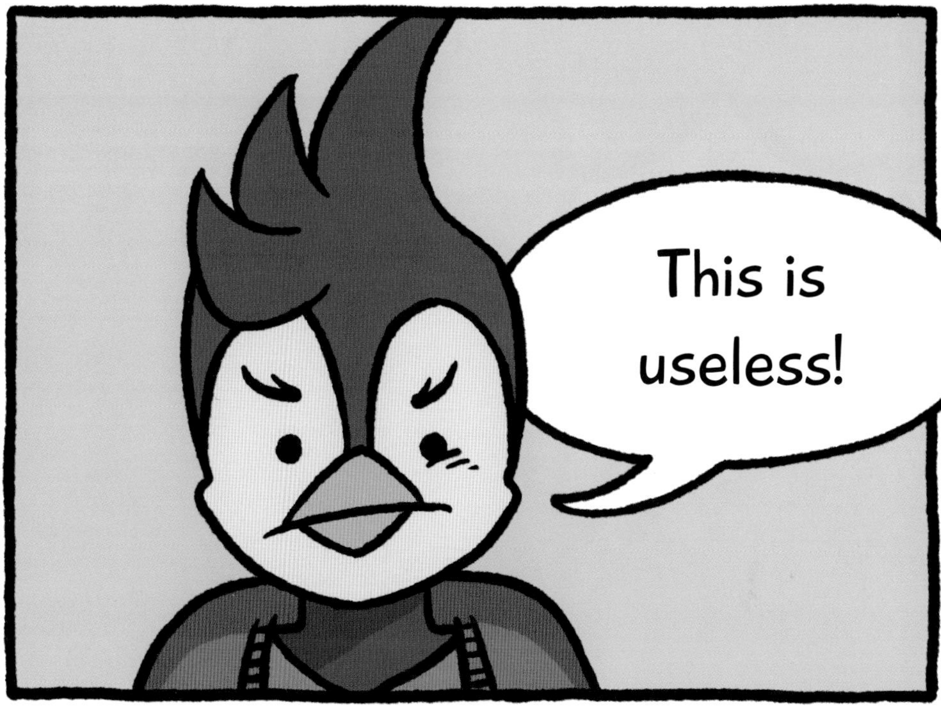
This is useless!

Pey-Pey hops away.

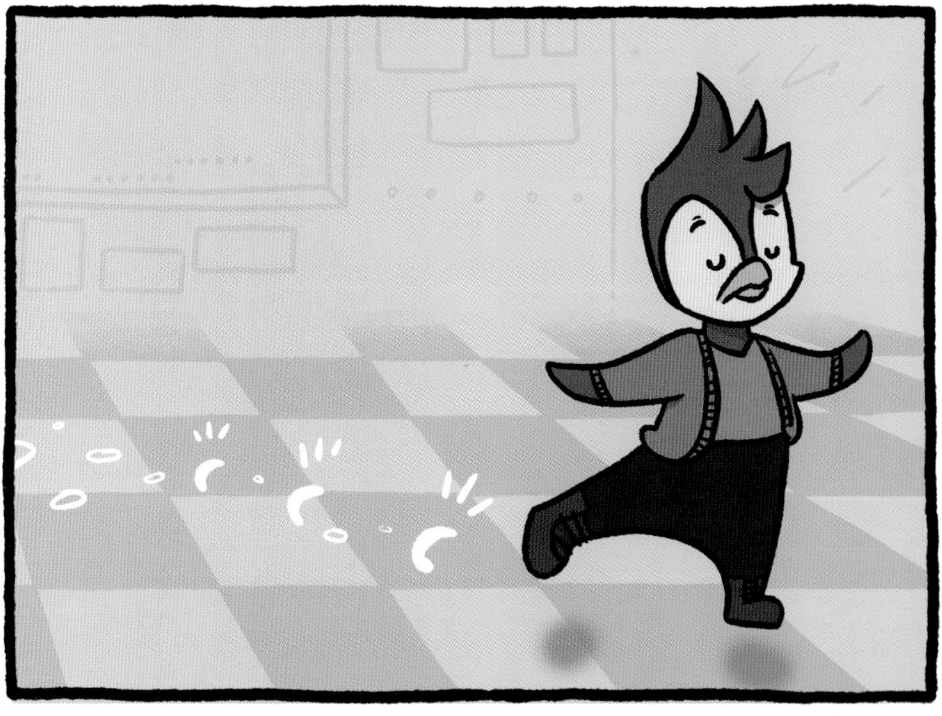

But then...

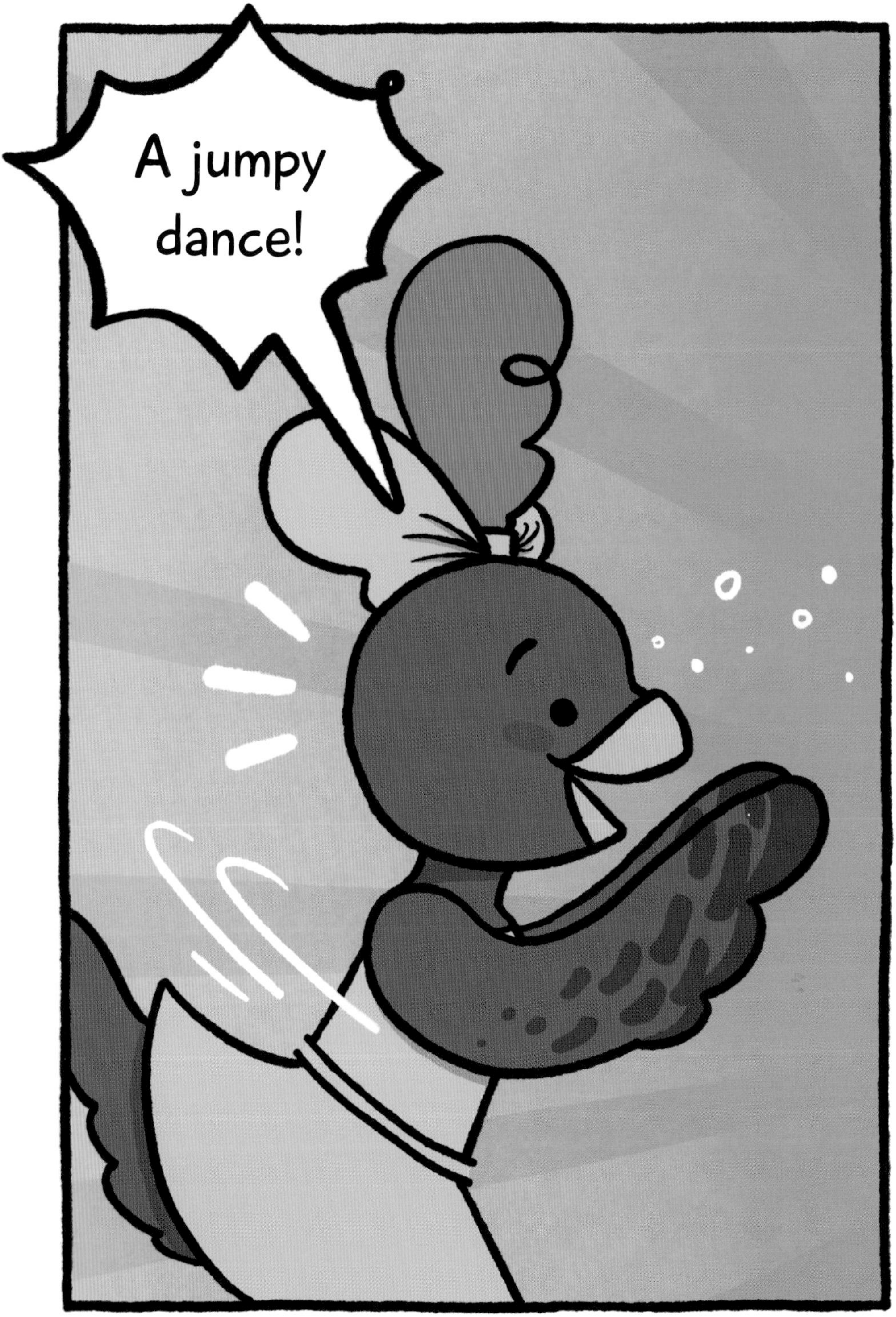
A jumpy dance!

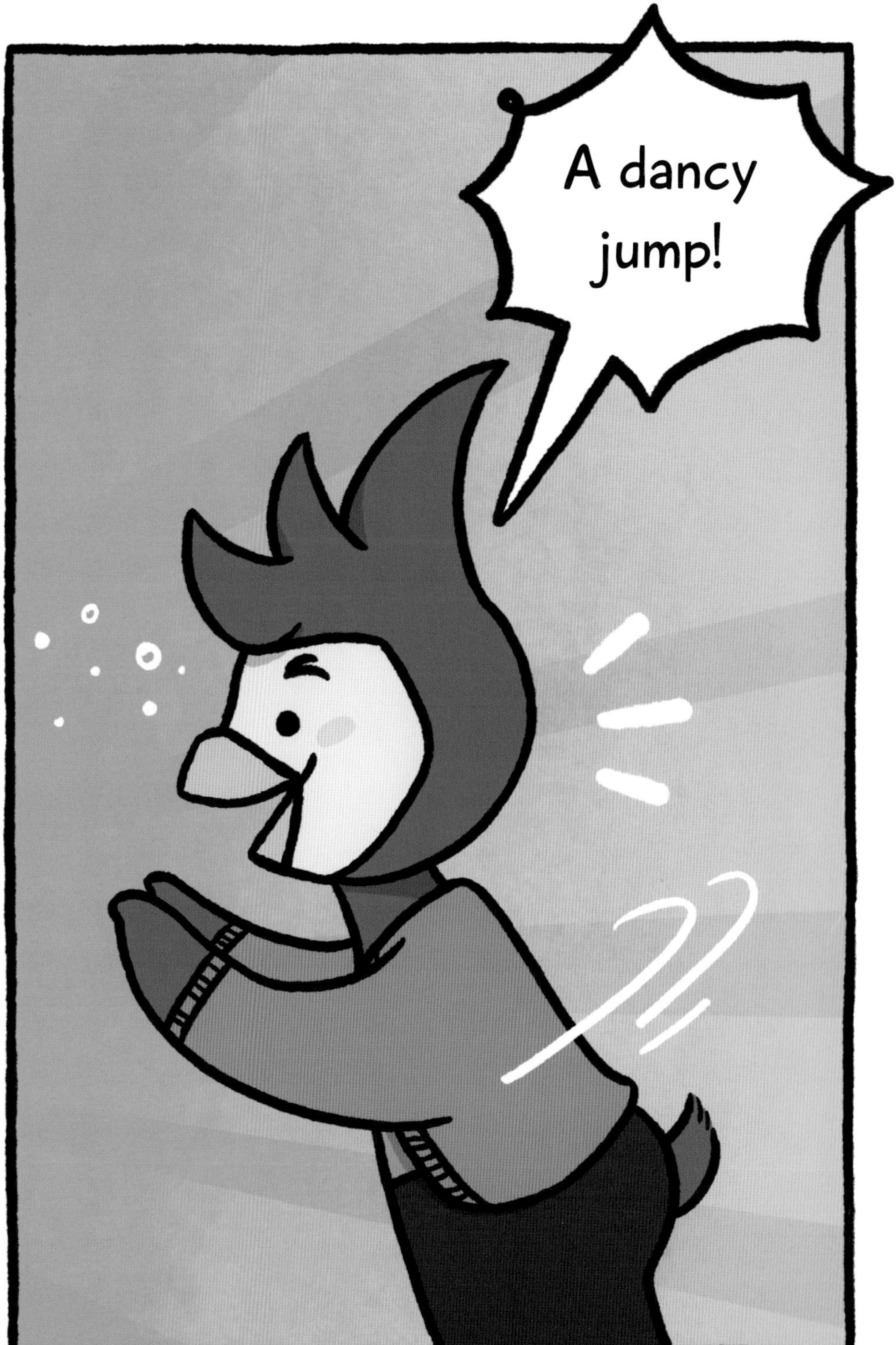
A dancy jump!

This is how exactly four minutes and three seconds after they meet...

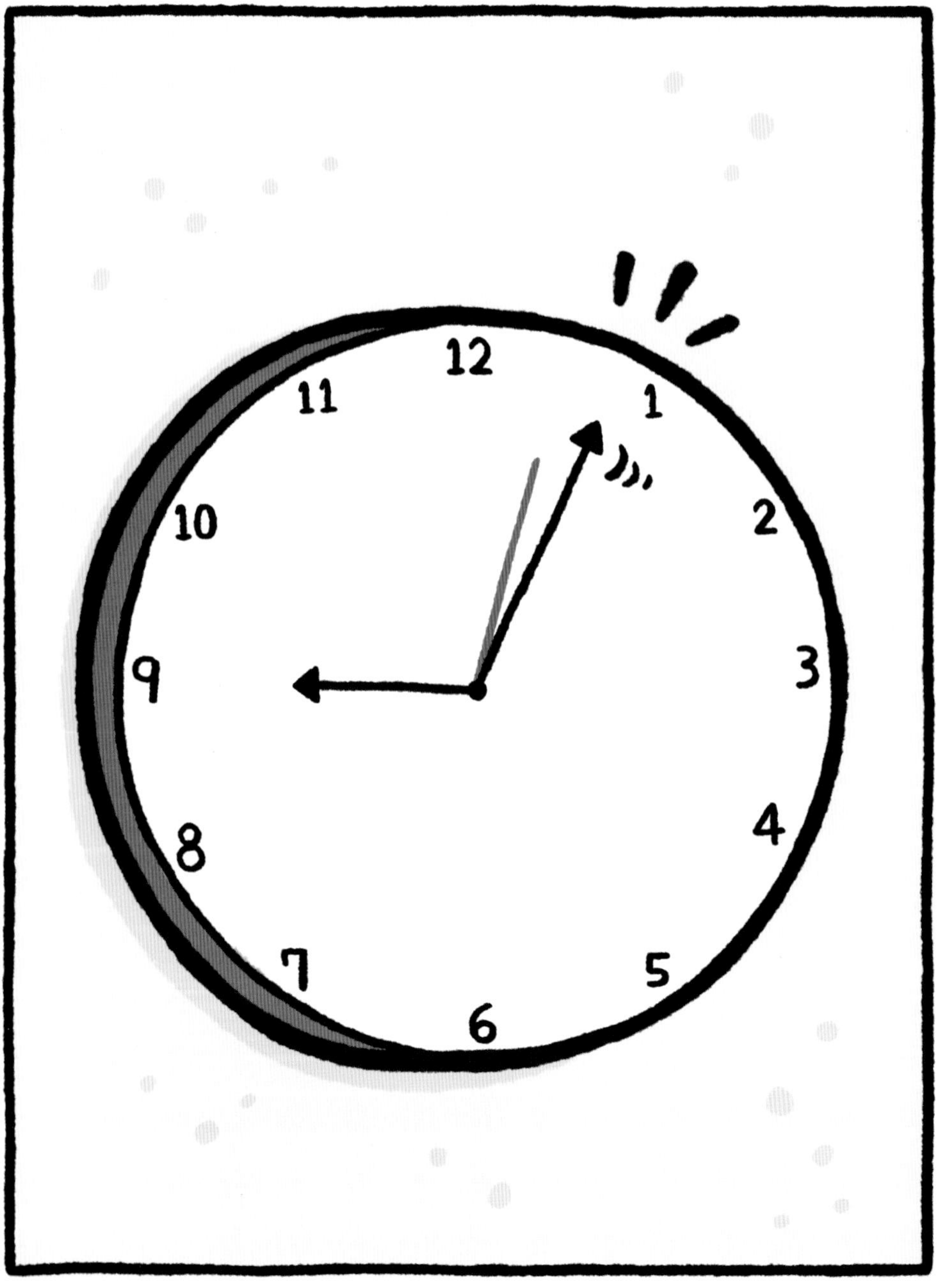

12
1
2
3
4
5
6
7
8
9
10
11

Chi-Chi and Pey-Pey become best friends.

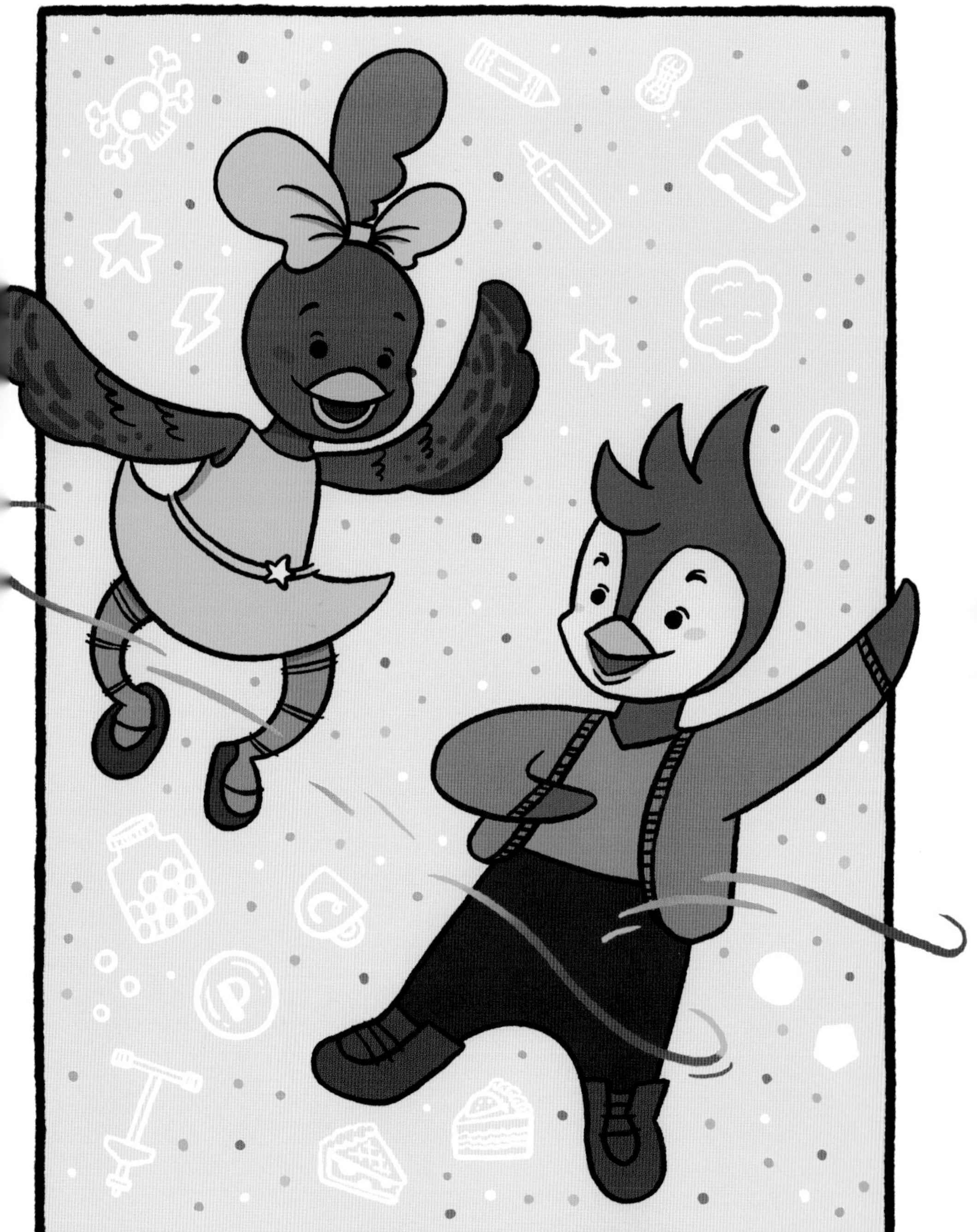

And Mrs. Possum's class learns to do the jumpy, dancy...

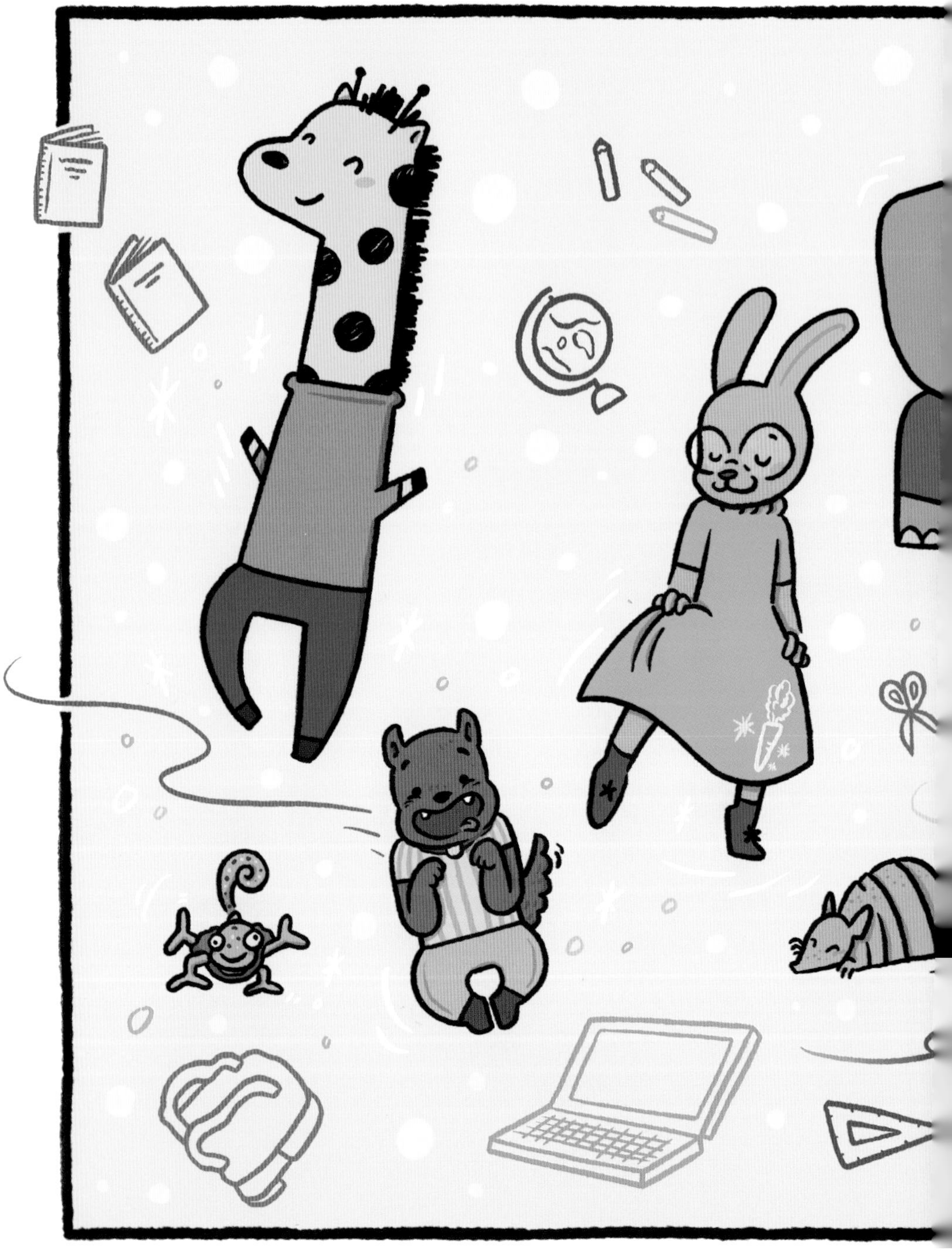

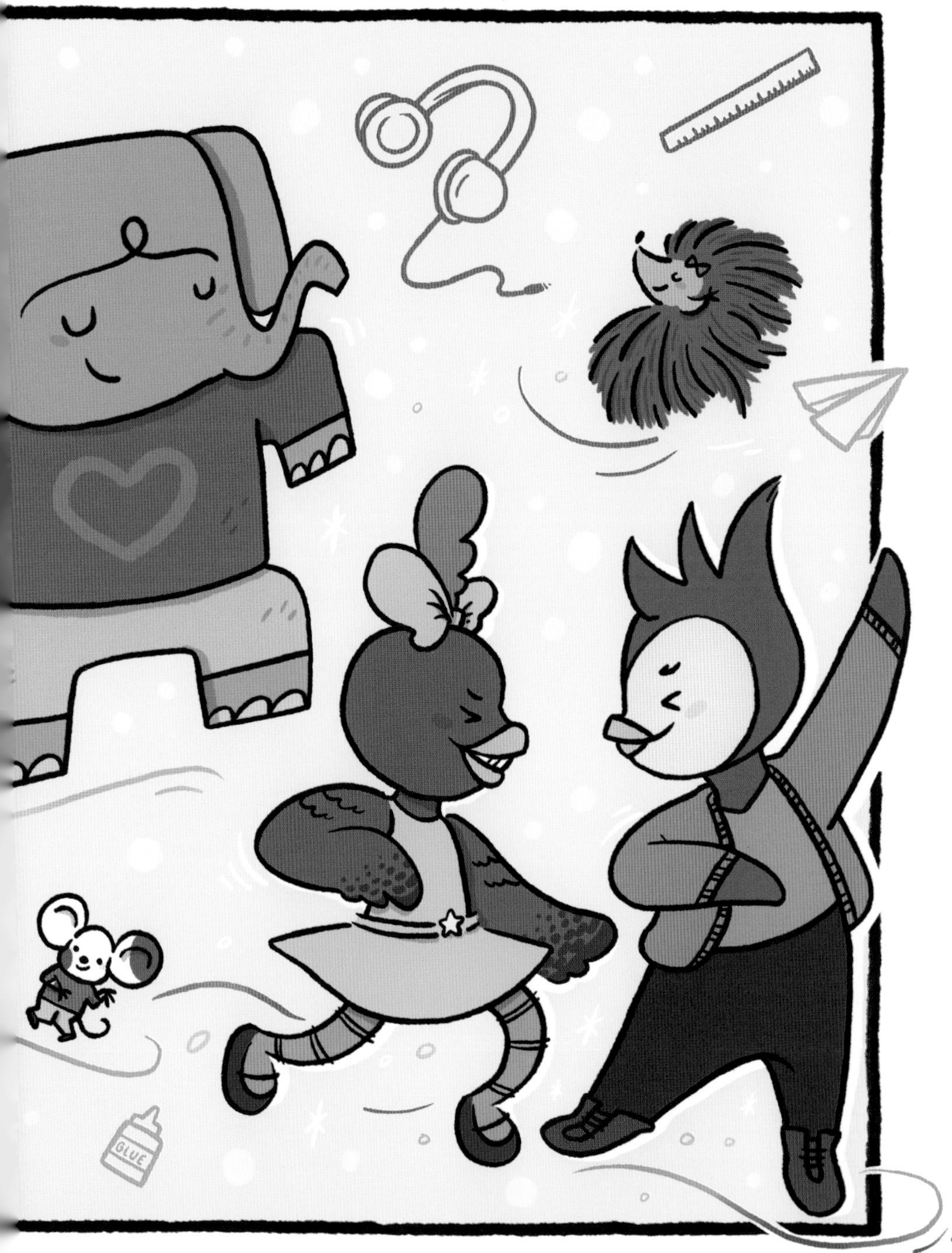
GLUE

...bunny hop!

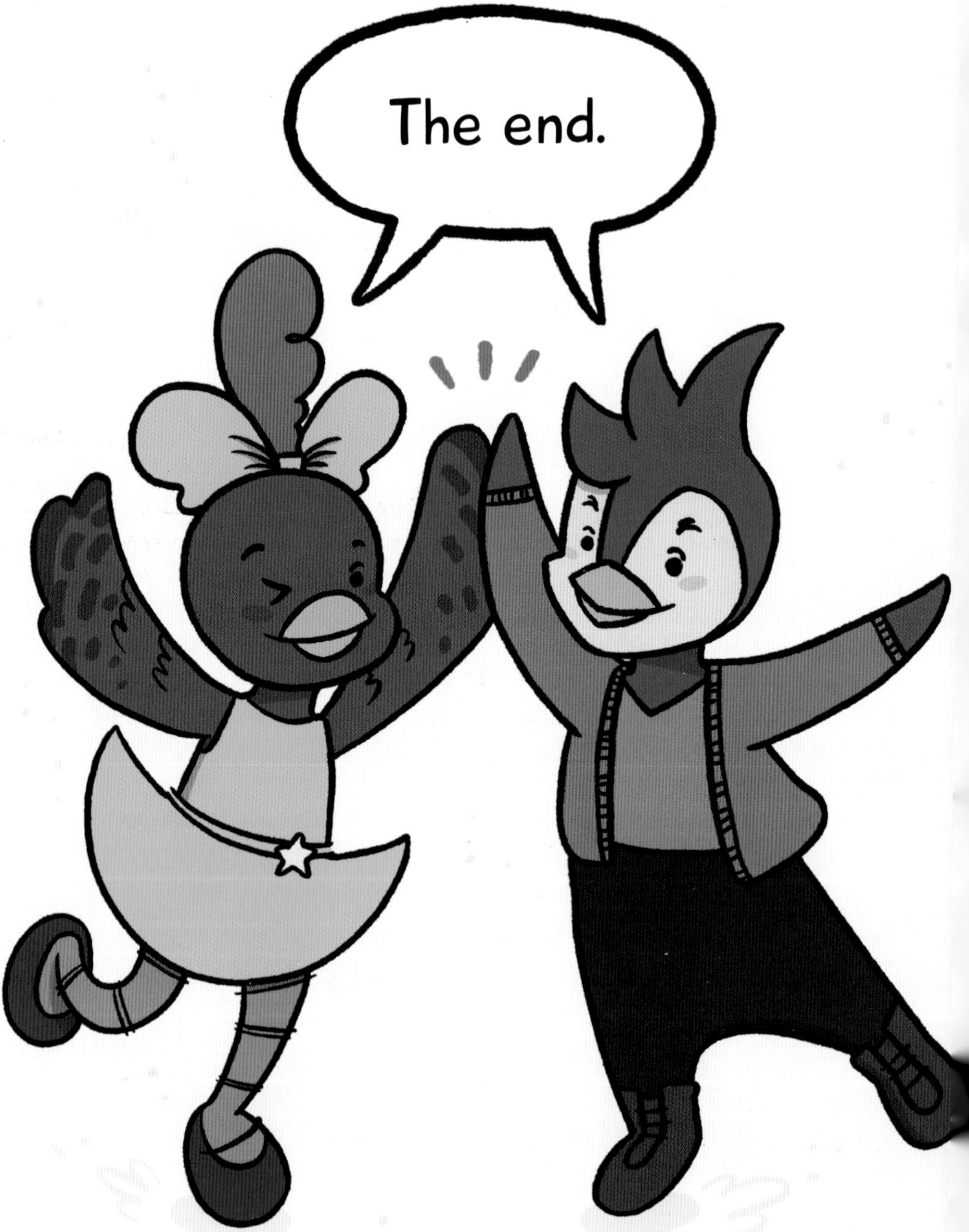
The end.